Happy New Year

Happy New Year

BY

TRACY WILSON

Published by
Beautiful Publications LLC
Stratford, CT 06614

Library of Congress Control Number:
2023900354
Print ISBN: 979-8-9871005-3-0
Ebook ISBN: 979-8-9871005-2-3

Printed in the United States of America

"Good morning…" Dana greeted…

"Good morning…" I greeted as I went over to my desk, turned on my computer, and took off my coat. Just as I sat my coffee on my desk, my director started her shit…

"I'm sorry to tell you this, but I'm afraid I can't approve your vacation next week…" I took the hanger off the hook, hung up my coat, sat down at my desk, and began drinking my coffee… "Did you hear what I said Chelle?"

"I heard you…"

"So you'll be here next week?"

"No I won't…"

"I just told you…"

"I already bought my tickets…" I interrupted…

"You need to get a refund or credit because I'm not approving your vacation..." I didn't bother responding. I continued sipping my coffee and opened my email. Just as I suspected, she had already clicked 'Not Approved' before I got into the office. I didn't even bother to take out my cell phone. I forwarded the email to Victoria in personnel and wrote the following:

"Good morning Victoria,

I am forwarding this email to you because unfortunately, Dana has just informed me that she will not be approving my vacation.

As you can see by the attached, I submitted my request six weeks ago. At no time was I informed my request wouldn't be approved. Dana never asked me to come into her office to discuss my request – in fact, the only response I received from her was a verbal "Chelle – I received your request." It wasn't mentioned again until this morning when she told me she couldn't approve it, after she denied my request in the system yesterday so that I would be sure to receive it via email first thing this morning.

Before I sat down to forward this email, I informed Dana that I already bought my tickets and her response was, "You need to get a credit or a refund because I'm not approving your vacation."

This situation is very disheartening. It's not just about losing money on the tickets – it's about how I'm valued as an employee in this agency. It saddens me to know that rather than have a discussion with me within six weeks, Dana waited until I left the office yesterday to deny my request to make sure I saw it first thing when I opened my email this morning.

I am going on vacation next week. I will be using four days AL from Tuesday through Friday, December 27th through December 30th, and one day AL on Tuesday, January 3rd. I will be returning to work on Wednesday, January 4th."

I made sure to cc Dana and sent the email. I went into my signature and set up the message reply so anyone that sent me an email would receive that message...

"Chelle – I need to see you in my office – NOW!!"

"Sorry Dana – I need to make sure I get these calendars out before I go on vacation..." I answered without getting up. Dana got up out her chair, stormed out of her office, and came up behind me...

"I SAID I NEED TO SEE YOU IN MY OFFICE – NOW!!" she boomed from behind me.

Everyone gathered around to see what would happen as I started shaking. I picked up the phone and dialed Victoria's number...

"Victoria – this is Chelle – Dana is yelling at me and demanding that I come into her office – I'm leaving for the day because she's being hostile and I feel threatened." I hung up the phone, turned off my computer, got up, put on my coat, and walked out...

"Hello?" I said as I answered my cell...

"Girl! What happened?" Veronica exclaimed...

"Damn – you heard huh?" I laughed...

"You alright?!"

"I'm okay..."

"You know she's gonna write you up – right?"

"Good luck with that..." I laughed...

"Oh shit – you really don't give a fuck!!"

"I do..."

"So you really quit?"

"I didn't quit..."

"Well – everybody's saying you quit..."

"Thank God that's a lie..." I sighed...

"Whew!! You had me worried..."

"Can you meet me at Haiku?"

"I can't leave until 12..."

"That's fine – I'll go to the Galleria and buy myself a present..."

"Alright – I'll see you at Haiku..."

Happy New Year

"Welcome to Kay Jewelers – I'm Cindy – how may I help you?"

"I need to reward myself for being a good girl..." I answered as I looked at the diamond bracelets...

"We have a sale going on now – the more you spend – the more you save..."

"How much for this bracelet?" I asked as I pointed to the $5k tennis bracelet on display..."

"That's a nice piece – if you want it you should put down a deposit – a few people have been in here already – in fact – someone is coming back later with her husband to have another look at it..."

"Really Cindy?" I asked as I gave her a look...

"Okay – you got me..." she sighed...

"I want the bracelet..."

"I know..."

"I want it today..."

"Really?" she asked as she perked up...

"Yes..."

"Okay!" she exclaimed as she opened the case... "Oh wow..." she whispered...

"What's wrong?"

"I forgot – this is 20% off..."

"Okay..." I replied, waiting for the other shoe to drop...

"So that's a thousand off..."

"Okay..." I replied as I pulled out the envelope I received...

"What's that?" she asked as if she didn't know...

"It's my new card with special offers, extra benefits, and zero down financing..." I answered as I smiled...

"Have you activated the card yet?"

"Not yet..."

"I can activate it for you if you like..."

"Okay..." I replied as I handed her the paper with my card on it...

"Oh my goodness – you must be a really good customer..." she beamed when she saw my credit limit...

"I am..."

"Well then – let's get this run up – you qualify for 36 months and zero financing – would you like to try this on before I box it up?"

"Yes..." I answered as I placed my wrist on the counter. Cindy put the bracelet on my wrist and I fell in love...

"Oh yes – I deserve this..." I sighed...

"It looks beautiful..." she sighed...

"Okay – that's it – take it off and put it in a box before I change my mind..."

"Oh no!"

"Relax – I'm buying it – I just want you to put it in a box so I don't wear it out the store..."

Happy New Year

"Oh thank God..." she sighed as she boxed it up for me and put it in a bag... "Merry Christmas and Happy New Year..."

"Merry Christmas and Happy New Year..." I replied as I took the bag and left to meet Veronica at Haiku...

"Welcome to Haiku – table for one?"

"Table for two..."

"Okay – come with me..." the hostess said as she picked up two menus. I followed her to the table and sat down... "Someone will be here to take your order in a few minutes..." she said before walking away. I looked around the restaurant and shook my head. There wasn't anyone else in the restaurant so I didn't understand why I had to wait...

"Welcome to Haiku – table for one?" I heard the hostess say...

"I'm meeting someone..." Veronica answered as she walked to our table and sat down...

"Can I get you something to drink?" the waiter asked as he took out his pad...

"I'll have ginger ale..."

"I'll have Pepsi..."

"Okay – I'll be right back..."

"I'm glad you asked me to come here..." Veronica said...

"Me too..."

"I already know what I want – I want prawn with mixed vegetables – white sauce – white rice..."

"That sounds good..." I said as the waiter came back to the table...

"What would you like?"

"Prawn with mixed vegetables – white sauce – white rice..." Veronica answered...

"I'll have the same..." I said...

"Would you like any appetizers?"

"Yes – I'd like an order of shumi – and two shots of vodka..."

"Would you like an appetizer Maam?" he asked as he turned to Veronica...

"Naa – I'm good..."

"Okay – I'll be right back..." he said as he left to place our order...

"So you didn't quit..."

"No..."

"Well what happened?"

"She denied my vacation..." I answered as the waiter put the shumi and vodka shots on the table...

"Oh shit! Did you get your money back?!"

"Nope..."

"You better than me – I'd go on vacation anyway – fuck that!!"

"I am..."

"Oh shit – I know she mad!"

"A toast..." I said as I raised my shot...

"What are we drinking to?"

"Bermuda..."

"Here's to Bermuda!" Veronica exclaimed and then we both drank our shots... "Damn that shit's strong!"

"I know..." I laughed as I started eating the shumi... "Well – don't just sit there – help me eat these!" I laughed...

"Shit – you ain't gotta tell me twice!" she exclaimed as she picked up her chop sticks and took one...

"How do you do that so easy?"

"It's not hard..." she answered as the waiter put our food on the table...

"Okay – so I went into work – Dana says good morning – I say good morning and I turn on my computer..."

"Okay..."

"I take off my coat, hang it up, sit down, and start drinking my coffee..."

"Okay..."

"I take one sip of my coffee and she says I'm sorry I can't approve your vacation..."

"Today?!"

"Yes..."

"She did that shit on purpose..."

"I know she did – that's why I ignored her..."

"Oh shit!"

"She asked me if I heard what she said – I told her I heard you and I kept right on drinking my coffee..."

"I know that's right!"

"So she goes in her office and as soon as I open my email I see unapproved on the request..."

"She did that shit last night!"

"I know she did – that's why I forwarded the email to Victoria in personnel and I cc'd her ass!"

"Oh shit – what'd she say?"

"I have no idea – I left before she had a chance to respond..."

"You should've stayed until she replied to your email..."

"I was going to stay the whole day but after what happened..."

"After what happened?!"

"Dana asked me if I heard what she said. I said yes, she said so you'll be here next week and I said no I won't..."

"Oh Shit!"

"So then she says I just told you – I cut her off and told her I already bought my tickets..."

"Right!"

"This Bitch gonna say I need to get a refund or a credit 'cause she's not approving my vacation..."

"Fuckin' bitch – she could 'a told you that yesterday before you left..."

"That's what I said in my email..."

"You did?"

"I sure did..."

"That's why she's mad..."

"That's not all I said..."

"Oh shit! What else did you say?""

"Well..." I began to answer as I finished my food... "I said she waited until yesterday to deny my request, she told me to get a refund or a credit, and she never discussed my request with me until this morning..."

"That's right!"

"And then I said the situation was disheartening and it made me sad because I didn't feel like a valued employee..."

"Well damn! I need to borrow that!"

"And then I ended the email letting her know that I will be using four days AL from Tuesday through Friday, December 27th through December 30th, and one day AL on Tuesday, January 3rd. I will be returning to work on Wednesday, January 4th and I cc'd Dana...

"Oh shit! She didn't call you in the office?"

"She did – but I told her I'm sorry I need to get the calendars out before I go on vacation..."

"Damn! I know she was mad!"

"She come out of her office, comes to my desk, and yells at the top of her lungs I said I need to see you in my office – now!!"

"Oh hell no – she would 'a got curse the fuck out!"

"I was so mad – I stood up and I started shaking..."

"You need to stand up to her..."

"I did..."

"You cursed her out?"

"Veronica – the last time that happened to me I went home crying..."

"WHAT?!"

"It wasn't Dana – I worked somewhere else..."

"So did you curse Dana out?!"

"Nope..."

"So how did you stand up to her then?!"

"I called Victoria's number, I said Dana was yelling at me, she was being hostile, and I was leaving for the day because I felt threatened..." Veronica dropped her chopsticks on her plate, pushed her chair back from the table, and stood up... "Where are you going?"

"I'm giving you a hug!" she exclaimed as she threw her arms around me and chocked me... "I can't breathe!" I laughed...

"I'm sorry..." she said as she sat back down... "I'm so proud of you!"

"I'm proud of me too – I'm so proud of myself I bought myself a present for being a good girl..."

"Oh shit – le'me see it!"

"Here it is..." I sighed as I handed her the bag...

"Oh my God! This is nice!"

"Thank you..."

"I've been a good girl too – can you buy me one?" she laughed...

"I wish I could..." I sighed...

"I'm just playin' – besides – I'll probably get one from Mr...."

"I thought you got your gift already?"

"Not yet – he told me I had to wait until next week..."

"I can't believe she told people I quit..."

"Did you clock out?"

"Oh shit – I forgot!"

"Don't worry about it – Vicky will take care of it..."

"Dana will tell her to put me LWP..."

"Vicky won't let her do that..."

"How do you know?"

"Since you left that message, Vicky won't let Dana put you out on LWP..."

"I'm still going on vacation..."

"Good..."

"I don't know what to expect when I get back though..."

"Worry about that when you come back..."

"Okay..."

"Are you packed?"

"Yea..."

"Already?"

"I'm only bringing a carry-on..."

"For a week?!"

"I'm going shopping when I get down there..."

"Le'me get back to work..." she sighed as she got up...

"I'll walk you..." I said as I got up...

"He didn't bring the check...

"He doesn't have to – as soon as we get to the front – they'll get it..." I said as I picked up my bag and we headed to the front...

"I'll get the check for you..." she said as she hurried to get the waiter...

"I'm learning a lot from you today..." Veronica said as the hostess brought the check... and she pulled out her credit card...

"Umm – excuse me – I invited you to lunch..."

"You can get next time..."

"Thank you..."

"You're welcome – c'mon..." she said as we hurried out the door...

"Enjoy your vacation – I'll see you when you get back..." I was just about to thank her when I saw Dana...

"Umm – thanks – I gotta go..." I stammered as I hurried down the block...

"Yes Dana..." Victoria sighed...

"I want Chelle put on administrative leave without pay for two weeks!"

"I can't do that..."

"I told her I wasn't approving her vacation and she left anyway – that's insubordination – I said..."

"Dana – let me stop you right there..."

"What?!"

"I know you're mad..."

"Ya think?!"

"Dana – you can't do anything to Chelle..."

"WATCH ME!"

"Dana – anything you do to Chelle will strengthen her complaint..."

"That Bitch filed a complaint?!"

"Not yet..."

"Are you telling me she can be insubordinate and I have to let her get away with it?!"

"Dana – I know you don't want to hear this..."

"I swear – you get on my fuckin' nerves – if I ran personnel I wouldn't tolerate any of this bullshit – I'd bounce people out on their ass!!"

"You can leave now..."

"Excuse me?!"

"I said you can leave now..."

"You're putting me out of your office?"

"Dana – please leave..."

"I'll leave when I'm good and damn ready!" Dana snapped as she sat down in the chair and crossed her legs. Victoria picked up the phone and dialed Kevin's number, and put the phone on speaker...

"Hello Vicky – what can I do for you?"

"You can come collect the trash..."

"Who the fuck you calling trash?!" Dana snapped as Kevin laughed in the background...

"I'm on my way..." he said as he hung up...

"I don't know who the fuck you think you are but let me tell you one fucking thing..."

"I get off work at 5 - If you need me to remind you who the fuck I am – meet me outside!" Dana continued to sit there as Victoria went in her desk drawer and pulled out Chelle's personnel file...

"Dana – what are you doing?" Kevin laughed as he walked into the office...

"I came in here to see..."

"Kevin – she needs to go – now!" Victoria interrupted...

"What happened?"

"I called you because I want this Bitch out of my office – if you can't handle it I'll handle it myself!" she snapped as she jumped up...

"Dana – let's go..." Kevin sighed. Dana reluctantly got up from the chair and took her time going towards the hallway...

"I'll see you later..." Dana said as she smiled and waved...

"Vicky – I'm..."

"Look – I'm not interested in your personal business – but when it affects my personnel business – that's a fuckin' problem!"

"You wanna tell me what happened?"

"I want you to sign this transfer request so I can transfer Chelle over to 85 Court Street..." she answered as she pushed the folder towards him. Kevin sat down and looked over the transfer request...

"Doesn't she report to Dana?"

"Yes..."

"Why are you transferring her to 85?"

"Because that Bitch opened up a can of bullshit that I can't close..." Victoria sighed as she pushed the email I forwarded to her in front of him. Kevin read the email and shook his head...

"I agree that Dana's actions weren't appropriate – but it's not enough for me to consider transferring Chelle..."

"Let me play you a message..." Victoria said as she hit the button...

"Victoria – this is Chelle – Dana is yelling at me and demanding that I come into her office – I'm leaving for the day because she's being hostile and I feel threatened."

"Shit!" Kevin exclaimed... "She knew what the fuck she was doing when she left that message!"

"Why do you always side with Dana? Is the pussy that good?!"

"Watch it Vicky!"

"Oh please –you ain't gonna do shit to me or Dana..." she said as she pushed the transfer request in front of him again...

"I'm not signing it..."

"Dana came to see me because she wanted me to put Chelle on administrative leave for two weeks without pay..."

"She can't do that..."

"I know she can't – and you know she can't – but even if she could – Chelle doesn't deserve that..."

"Dana must have a bug up her ass..."

"She does – Chelle sent her a copy of the email..."

"See?! I told you that Bitch knew what the fuck she was doing!"

"Why is Chelle the Bitch?! Why isn't Dana – never mind – hurry up and sign this request so I can process her transfer..."

"I'm not signing it..."

"Fine – don't sign it – but when Chelle and I file a complaint – remember our conversation..."

"Chelle and you?!"

"Dana threatened me before I called you..."

"Are you serious?"

"She told me I get on her fuckin' nerves because I always side with the employees – and then she said if she were the head of personnel she'd bounce people out on their ass!"

"That's not a threat..."

"If I perceive it as a threat – it's a threat – and that's not all she said..."

"What else did she say?"

"After I called you she said she don't know who the fuck I think I am but let her tell me something..."

"Okay, okay – I get it..."

"I'm not finished..."

"I'm sorry – Please – Continue..."

"I told her I get off at 5 and if she needed me to remind her who I was she can meet me outside..."

"Vicky! Why would you say that?!"

"I asked her to leave my office and she told me she'd leave when she's good and damn ready..."

"I swear – I wish she'd learn to shut her fuckin' mouth sometimes..." he laughed...

"If you put your dick in her mouth more often she might learn to..."

"Give me the damn request!" he laughed as he snatched the request and signed it...

"Thank you..."

"You lucky I like you..."

"Whatever..."

"You know I gotta tell her – right?"

"You don't have to tell her a damn thing – you want to tell her!"

"That's not all I want..."

"EWW! I'm not listening – LA LA LA LA..." she sang as she covered her ears. Kevin shook his head as he got up and left the office...

"Yes Victoria..." Stephen answered...

"I have good news..."

"Oh? Do tell..."

"You're getting an Administrative Assistant..."

"I am?! When?!"

"She's on vacation next week – she'll report to you on Wednesday, January 4th..."

"Who is she? Do I know her?"

"You might – her name is Chelle Robinson..."

"Chelle Robinson? Doesn't she work at 112?"

"Not anymore..."

"Oh no – is she a trouble maker?"

"Have a nice weekend Stephen..." Victoria said as she was about to hang up...

"WAIT!!"

"Yes Stephen?"

"Thank you..."

"You're welcome..."

"Does she know yet?"

"Not yet – I'm going to let her know now..."

"Okay – have a nice weekend..."

"You too..."

"Shit!" I exclaimed when I saw the number on my phone... "Good afternoon..."

"May I speak with Chelle Robinson?"

"This is she..."

"Hi Chelle – this is Victoria from Personnel..."

"Hi Victoria..." I sighed...

"I won't keep you – I know you're about to leave for vacation – I just wanted to let you know your transfer's been approved..."

"Oh shit – I mean – sorry..." I laughed...

"That's okay – you'll be reporting to Stephen Richards at 85 Court Street on Wednesday, January 4th at 9 a.m...."

"Oh wow – okay!"

"You'll need to clean out your desk before you go if you want your stuff..."

"Oh shoot – I'm leaving tomorrow..."

"Is there any way you can go clean out your desk before you leave?"

"You want me to come in on Saturday?"

"You don't have to – I just figured you'd want your stuff..."

"Okay · I'll figure it out – thanks for the good news..."

"You're welcome – enjoy your vacation..."

"Oh I will – thank you again!"

"You're welcome..."

"Hello…" Veronica answered…

"Girl – I need your help…"

"I hope you don't need money!" she laughed…

"I need you to go clean out my desk…"

"What?! Why?!"

"I just talked to Victoria…"

"Oh shit – you lost your job?!"

"No – I got transferred…"

"See – that's that bullshit – why didn't they transfer Dana?!"

"Because I requested it a few months ago…"

"Okay so why can't you go clean out your desk before you leave?"

"Because as soon as Dana finds out I'm being transferred, she'll throw everything in the garbage..."

"When do you start?"

"I start the day I come back..."

"Wednesday?"

"Yup..."

"I still don't see why you need me to clean out your desk for you..."

"Because I don't want to clean out my desk tomorrow..."

"On Saturday?"

"Yea..."

"Okay – I'll go clean out your desk – but you're gonna meet me to pick up your box – right?"

"Could you put it on your desk until I get back?"

"When are you picking up your box?"

"As soon as I find out where my desk is..."

"So you're gonna wait all day until you find out where you're sitting before you come get your box?"

"I'm pretty sure Stephen will show me where I'll be sitting as soon as I get there..."

"Stephen?! Stephen Richards?!"

"Yup!"

"Oh shit – I know where you'll be sitting – you'll be sitting right next to me!"

"Okay!"

"I'll go clean out your desk now..."

"Thank you girl!"

"You're welcome – I'll see you when you get back..."

"Okay – don't tell anybody – Dana doesn't know yet..."

"Oh shit – okay!"

"Hello Veronica – are you looking for Chelle?" Dana asked as Veronica came inside...

"No – she left something on her desk..." Veronica answered as she headed towards my desk with a box. Dana got up from her chair and came out by my desk...

"Well damn – you sure are filling that box up – what did Chelle forget?!"

"Everything..." Veronica answered as she finished packing the box and put the top on it...

"Is Chelle outside?"

"I have no idea where Chelle is..." Veronica answered as she picked up the box... "Could you get the door for me?"

"Sure..." Dana answered as she went to open the door, opened it, and held it open...

"Thanks – have a Happy New Year y'all..." Veronica said as she walked out the door without looking back...

"Five o'clock – time to go check this Bitch!' Dana snapped as she put on her coat, picked up her pocketbook, turned off her computer, and left the office...

"Hello Dana..." Victoria greeted as she walked up towards Dana...

"We ain't inside now – you said you gonna remind me who the fuck you are – right?!"

"I did..."

"Well? I don't see you doing shit!"

"Happy New Year Dana..." Victoria said as she handed Dana an envelope. Dana snatched it, opened it, and began reading. Victoria smiled as her eyes got really big...

"You think this is over?! Watch what happens on Tuesday!!"

"It's over Dana – Kevin approved it – I'll fill your vacancy as soon as I get back from vacation – have a Happy New Year!" she exclaimed as she waved at Dana and then turned to leave...

"Hey..." Kevin sighed...

"You wanna tell me why you signed Chelle's transfer request?"

"What time is it Dana?"

"It's after 5 – but..." Kevin held up a box wrapped in red paper with a big gold bow on it...

"You were saying?"

"Never mind!" she exclaimed as she walked over to the desk and tried to take the present from him...

"Uh Uh!" he snapped as he pulled the box away from her. Dana began to pout and he bust out laughing...

"It's not funny..."

"Yes it is!" he laughed again...

"Can I have my present? Please?"

"I'll think about it..." Dana went over to the door, locked it, and went to sit down on the sofa...

"Are you almost done?"

"I'm almost done..." he answered without looking up from his work. He knew Dana was annoyed and he smiled to himself. Dana pulled a red box with a green bow on it out of her bag and sat it beside her on the sofa...

"I wish we could spend Christmas together..." she sighed...

"We have all day tomorrow..."

"I know... I just wish things were different..."

"That's not happening..."

"I know... I just wish it could happen..." Kevin put his papers in his desk, closed the drawer, got up, picked up the gift he had for her, and went to sit down beside her...

"You'd really leave your husband for me?"

"I've thought about it..."

"I think it's best to leave things as they are..."

"So you never thought about leaving your wife?"

"Dana – I don't want to hurt you..."

"So you don't love me?"

"Dana..." he sighed as he took her hand... "I do love you..."

"I love you too..."

"My wife knew who I was before she married me..."

"I don't understand..."

"I let my wife know I could never commit to just one woman..."

"And she's okay with that?!"

"She doesn't have a choice..."

"You gave her an ultimatum?!"

"I gave her a choice – and she chose to accept me as I am..."

"Oh hell no – I could never do that..."

"You could never do that but you expect your husband to..."

"That's different..."

"How?"

"He doesn't know..."

"He knows..."

"What makes you say that?"

"A man always knows..."

"Are you ready to go?" she asked, deliberately changing the subject...

"That depends..." he breathed as he pulled her into a kiss...

"Mmm..."

"Do you want your gift now..." he breathed as he began kissing her down her neck... "Or do you want your gift at the hotel?"

"I want..."

"Yesss..."

"I want my gift at the hotel..."

"Are you sure?" he breathed as he kissed her again...

"Yeesss..."

"Why can't we have a little fun here?"

"Because..." she breathed between kisses... "Once you start... I don't wanna stop..."

"Okay – c'mon..." he said as he stood up and extended his hand to help her up. Dana put his gift back in her bag, he picked up Dana's gift, they unlocked the door, and then they left the office...

"Hey Veronica..." I answered...

"I got it..."

"Thank you..."

"You know she tried it – right?"

"I knew she would..." I laughed...

"She asked me if you were waiting outside – I told her I had no idea where you were..." she laughed...

"Did she ask why you were cleaning out my desk?"

"I told her you left something on your desk - she said damn – you sure are filling up that box – what did she forget – I said everything – and

31

then I asked her to get the door for me!" she laughed...

"Did she get the door for you?"

"She sure did – I said thanks and Happy New Year! Ahh haa haa haa!"

"You have made my night girl!"

"You sure you don't wanna go out for a drink?"

"I can't – my flight leaves tomorrow morning at 6 a.m...."

"Oh shit – you don't wanna be here for Christmas?"

"Nope..."

"Shit – how much was your flight?"

"Eleven eighteen..."

"Round trip?!"

"Yup..."

"You leaving from LaGuardia?"

"No – I'm leaving from White Pains..."

"Nice!"

"I can't wait to get down there and spend the week on the beach in nothing but my G-string bikini..."

"G-string?! Not you!!" she laughed...

"Why not me?"

"I need pictures!"

"Nope!"

"You ain't right!"

"I'll take some pictures... of some things..."

"Oh... I get it..."

"I know you do – and I'ma get mine too!" I laughed...

"Oh shit! Le'me find out!" she laughed...

"I'm looking for Dexter!" I laughed...

"Dexter gonna have your ass soakin' in some Epsom salt – you better be careful!" she laughed...

"I'll take my chances!" I laughed...

"Don't stop..." Dana moaned...

"You like this dick — don't you!" Kevin growled...

"I love it!" Kevin laid down on her back and continued pounding her from behind... "Fuck! Just like that! Don't stop! I'm cumming!"

"Uggh! Uggh! Uggh! Uggh! UUUGGGHHH!" They both fell down on the bed and Kevin laid on top of her for a few moments...

"You're still hard..." she breathed...

"I know..." he breathed in her ear before he turned over on his back...

"Let me handle that..." Dana said as she got up on her knees, spread Kevin's legs, and got in between them. Kevin put his hands behind his head as she bent down towards his dick and then she put her tongue on the tip of it...

34

"Don't tease me..."

"Why not?" she asked and then she started licking the shaft. Kevin held her head on both sides, closed his eyes, and started playing in her hair. Dana knew that was her que to take his dick in her mouth...

"FUCK..." Dana loved to hear him moan and each time he moaned, she turned it up a notch... "Yeess... suck it..." he moaned as he played in her hair. Kevin pushed her head down on his dick and began fucking her mouth... "Uggh! Uggh! Uggh! Uggh! UUUGGGHHH!" Dana swallowed and continued sucking softly for a few moments... "Damn..."

"You're welcome..."

"Let me give you your gift..." he sighed as he sat up...

"What's your hurry?"

"I'm not in a hurry – I just wanna see if you like it..." he answered as he got up out the bed...

"Okay..." Dana sat up, got out the bed, went over to her bag, took his gift out, and sat on the bed with the gift in her hand. Kevin sat down beside her...

"On three... one... two..."

"Three!" they both said as they exchanged boxes. Kevin opened his box first...

"Oh wow – this is nice! He exclaimed as he took the stainless steel diamond bracelet out the box...

"You really like it?"

"Yes!" he exclaimed as he looked over the links of stainless steel adorned with blue stainless steel cable and diamonds...

"Good..."

"What made you think I wouldn't like it?"

"The diamonds..."

"This is nice – it's not over the top – and blue is my favorite color..." he said as he put it on...

"It looks really good on you..."

"Open your gift – I wanna see if you like it!"

"Okay, okay!" she exclaimed as she opened the box... "Oh you got jokes..." she laughed sarcastically as she took the Citizen Disney Villains Evil Queen women's watch out the box...

"You don't like it?"

"You know I like the Evil Princess..." she answered as she looked at the engraving on the back... "I love the pin too..." she sighed as she picked up the heart and dagger pin in gunmetal grey, accented with gold-tone finishes including crystal details on the heart and a ruby-tone jewel...

"I'm glad you like it..."

"Thank you..." she breathed as she pulled him into a kiss...

"You're welcome..."

"What's wrong?"

"We need to talk..."

"Please... Don't..."

"Dana..."

"It was fun while it lasted..."

"What are you talking about?!" he snapped...

"It's over – right?"

"I thought you knew me better than that!"

"I'm sorry – you said we need to talk... so..."

"So you thought I brought you here to fuck you, end it, and give you a parting gift?!"

"I'm sorry..."

"No – I'm sorry – let's try this again – we need to talk about what happened earlier..."

"Oh my God – this is about Chelle?!"

"Yes..."

"Okay... Go ahead..."

"You can't do that again..."

"What'd I do?"

"Dana – don't try to insult my intelligence..."

"You're right – I'm sorry..."

"What are you sorry for?"

"Excuse me?"

"What are you sorry for?"

"I'm sorry for how I acted with Victoria..."

"Are you really sorry?"

"No... But I'm sorry you got put in the middle of it..."

"Exactly – especially since she knows we're fucking..."

"WHAT?!"

"Oh please – don't act surprised – you didn't exactly help the situation when you refused to leave her office and you continued to sit there until I asked you to leave!"

"Damn – now I have to be nice to her..."

"See – that's what I mean – you should be nice to her period!"

"Why – because she's your friend?" Kevin shook his head back and forth...

"Dana – your behavior is going to hurt us personally and professionally..."

"Okay – I got it..."

"If you really got it as you say – then act like it!"

"Hey!"

"Look..." he said as he took her hand... "I'm enjoying this... I love what we have... but we can't jeopardize our jobs – the last thing we need is an enemy in personnel..."

"You're right..." she signed...

"What happened in the parking lot?"

"How'd you know about that?"

"She told me..."

"Did she tell you what she did?"

"I know what she did..."

"Why'd you sign Chelle's transfer request?"

"I just told you – the last thing we need is an enemy in personnel..."

"So you're on Victoria's side..."

"Dana – could you get out of your head for a minute?!"

"What's that supposed to mean?!"

"What do you think would've happened if I didn't sign her transfer request?"

"She would've come back to work – she would've been pissed off but she would've gotten over it..."

"That's not all that would've happened and you know it..."

"So I'm just supposed to let her go?"

"Dana – do you love me?"

"Yes..."

"Do you want us to keep seeing each other?"

"Are you giving me an ultimatum?"

"Answer the question..."

"Yes... I want us to keep seeing each other..."

"I want that too..." he breathed as he pulled her into a kiss... "And I also want to have a Merry Christmas..." he breathed as he kissed her neck... "A Happy New Year..." he breathed as he bit her earlobe... "And I want you to let this go so we can both continue to have our cake..." he breathed as he pushed her down on her back... "And eat it too..." he breathed as he spread her legs and dove in...

"Hello Mr. Tompkins..." Cindy greeted...
"I'm here to buy that tennis bracelet..."
"Oh shoot – I'm sorry – it's been sold..."
"Oh no!"

"We have some other bracelets you might like..." she said as she went over to the display case... "How's this?" she asked as she picked up the 1ct round-cut 10k rose gold 7 inch bracelet...

"It's lovely..." he sighed as he took it from her and held it. Cindy smiled as he examined each diamond... "This... this is the one..." he sighed...

"Great! I'll get this wrapped up for you!" she exclaimed as she took the bracelet from him and went to box it up. Darnell was beaming as he got a call on his cell...

"Hello Conrad..."

"Hello Darnell..."

"I was wrong about her – right?"

"I'm going to send you a picture..." he answered and then he hung up. Darnell looked at his phone and tears came to his eyes as he looked at the picture...

"Oh my God! What's wrong?!" Cindy exclaimed as she dropped the bag and rushed over to him. Darnell didn't bother answering her as he shoved his phone across the display case... "Is that your wife?" whispered...

"Yes..." he whispered as tears streamed down his face...

"I'm so sorry..." Cindy whispered as she gave Darnell a box of tissues...

"Are you married?" he asked as he dabbed his eyes...

"No..."

"Will you marry me?" he asked as he picked up a 10k rose gold engagement ring with a round diamond in the center set in white gold, haloed by round diamonds. Additional round diamonds dazzled and weaved through the band bringing the total diamond weight to ¼ carat...

"That's from our Now & Forever Collection..." she whispered...

"Now & Forever... that's perfect..." he said as he held the ring up and continued to look at it...

"Would you like the complementing wedding band?"

"Would you like it?"

"I don't understand..."

"I'm asking you... as a woman... if I proposed to you... with this ring... from the Now & Forever Collection... would you marry me?"

"Yes... I'd marry you..." Darnell pulled Cindy's face to his and kissed her in the mouth so fast and hard, it startled her... "Mr. Tompkins – Umm..."

"I'm sorry – I didn't mean to do that – actually I did – but I'm sorry if you're offended..."

"I'm not offended... I'm flattered..."

"Good... "

"I'll go get the complimenting wedding band and I'll put the tennis bracelet back..."

"I still want the bracelet..."

"You do?!"

"I do..."

"Okay..." Darnell waited for her to bag everything up. When he reached for the bag, she touched his hand...

"I'm sorry..."

"Thank you..."

"Your wife's a lucky woman..."

"What makes you say that?"

"You're still buying her a tennis bracelet even though you just found out she's cheating on you..."

"I'm not giving that bracelet to my wife..."

"You're not?!"

Happy New Year

"Naa – I'm giving the bracelet to my Now & Forever – I'm on my way to see my attorney – my wife will be served before Christmas and I'll be a free man before the New Year..." he answered on his way out the store...

"I can't wait to get this done..." he sighed as he sat down at his computer. After a few google searches, he found what he was looking for... "Uncontested Divorce – Printable Forms..." he said out loud as he clicked on the link... "I'll just print these out, fill them out, and leave them here for her to read over along with this picture..." he said as he printed the pages. Once he was done printing the papers, he emailed the picture to himself, opened his email, and printed the picture in color... "Wow Dana – I had no idea Kevin treated you so nice – I wonder how his wife would feel about this?" he asked as he contemplated forwarding the picture to Kevin's wife, Kenya... "You know what – Kenya's innocent in this – why should I ruin her Christmas..." he sighed. Darnell put the printed picture to the side, took out a pad and pen, and began writing...

"Dana,

I've thought something was wrong between us for a while, but I ignored the signs. Each time I wanted to be affectionate and you pulled away, I told myself you were tired or it was a side effect of your medication. The few times you actually let me make love to you – if you can call it that – I noticed you faked your orgasms – but again, I told myself you were tired or it was a side effect of your medication. I even justified what I told myself by googling the side effects of taking lithium and Risperdal while drinking alcohol and I was relieved to find out that one of the main side effects was drowsiness. It never bothered me that you were bipolar and schizophrenic because I fell in love with you before you told me and I continued to love you even after I found out.

I went to see Conrad because I needed to be wrong. I needed him to tell me that he became bored following you because the only thing he'd be watching you do was go to work, go to some meetings after work, and come home. Now that I've seen this picture of you and Kevin, I realize Conrad wasn't bored at all – he was entertained by your performance. Now that I've seen this picture, I'm sure there are others but I'm also sure that he didn't send them to me because he wants to spare my feelings.

Happy New Year

I went to Kay Jewelers earlier today to pick up that diamond tennis bracelet you had your eye on but fortunately, it was purchased by someone else – someone who was probably a lot more deserving than you. I picked out a beautiful alternative in rose gold and round diamonds – in fact, I actually thought you'd like it more than the one you wanted – and just as I was about to pay for it – I got the phone call from Conrad, followed by the picture – and guess what? Not only did I buy the bracelet – I also bought an engagement ring and wedding band from their Now & Forever Collection, I asked Cindy if she would marry me, and when she said yes – I kissed her!

I'm going to give the bracelet, engagement ring, and wedding band to the woman that will love me now and forever. Hopefully I'll find her when I touch down after I get off the plane. Since I won't be spending Christmas with you or bringing in the New Year with you, I'm leaving on the first flight I can get.

Do us both a favor and sign the divorce papers. If you would file them at the courthouse while I'm gone - that'd be great. If not – I'll do it myself when I get back.

Darnell"

Darnell put the pad to the side and began filling out the divorce papers. When he was finished, he put them alongside the letter, took his wedding band off, and put his wedding band on top of the divorce papers along with a pen...

"Fuck him..." he mumbled as he opened his email, attached the picture, and hit send... "Now... let's see what's poppin' tomorrow morning..." he said as he went to the White Plains Airport website... "Hmm... Bermuda... I think that's a nice place to start searching for my Now & Forever..." he said as he looked at the flights... "Hmm... 6 a.m.... a layover in Atlanta... I'll be in Bermuda at 1:30 p.m.... Sold!" he exclaimed as he took out his Amex card... "You won't be able to check for this one Dana..." he said as he booked the flight... "Hmm... I won't be back until Tuesday night at 10:30 p.m. – oh well – at least I'll be in White Plains..." he said as he completed his booking... "Now I just need to book a hotel, pack a bag, and get the hell out of here..." he sighed as he went to hotels.com and looked at their recommendations... "Hmm... Radison Grenada Beach Resort – 8 out of 10 stars – over 1k reviews, king-size bed, private balcony facing the beach, in my price range, and all the pussy, ass, and titties a man can ask for..." he sighed as he slid down in the chair and began rubbing his dick through his pants... "Le'me hurry up and book this room so I can get packed..." he said as he completed the booking, printed it, folded it, and put it in his pocket... "Now let me get my carry on, add some swimming trunks, a thong or two, and I'll be on my way..." he said as he got up and went to get the carry on. It didn't take long for Darnell to pack his carry on and when he was done, he went to sit back down at the computer... "I'm getting a room – I don't wanna see this Bitch when she gets the gifts I left for her..." he said as he went back to hotels.com and booked a room at Cambria... "Done – I won't even print it – but what I will do is log out so Dana won't know where I am..." he said as he logged out, turned off the computer, picked up his carry on, and left...

"Why am I getting an email from Darnell Tompkins?" Kenya asked as she opened the email... "Oh hell no!!"

"Don't stop Kevin..." Dana moaned as he continued licking, slurping, and sucking. Dana grabbed his head with both hands and her legs trembled as she rode his face... "I'M CUMMING!! AAAHHH!!" Kevin continued to devour her as her orgasm crescendoed and when she tried to push him off, he gripped her ass hard...

"Take it!!" he growled as he went back to working his tongue and lips on her clit...

"KEVIN... OH SHIT... I CAN'T!!" she panted. Kevin began shaking his head back and forth as she screamed again... "AAAHHH!!" Dana squirted all over his face as he continued to lick and suck softly...

"That's more like it..." he breathed as he looked up at her and wiped his face...

"Shit..." she sighed...

"What's wrong?"

"Your phone's vibrating..." she answered as she sat up. Kevin got up, went over to the nightstand, picked up his phone, and answered it...

"This is Kevin..."

"You need to come home..."

"I'm on my way..."

"What's wrong?"

"I need to go..." he answered as he started getting dressed. Dana knew better than to ask any more questions. She sat there in bed under the blanket as Kevin put his suit jacket on...

"Your bracelet..."

"What about it?"

"I thought you'd take it off..."

"I'll see you later..." he said as he left the room, closed the door, and went towards the elevator. The doors opened and he hurried inside without looking up...

"Excuse me..."

"Oh – my bad – oh hey Darnell..."

"Hello Kevin – tell your wife I said hello..."

"I sure will – Merry Christmas and Happy New Year..."

"Same to you Kevin..." Darnell said as he got off the elevator. The doors closed and Darnell smiled to himself as he went down the hall to his room and opened the door... "This is just right..." he sighed as he went to sit on the loveseat... "Let's see where my lovely wife is..." he said as he logged into the google maps feature and entered her number... "Well, well – lookee here..." he said as he saw that her phone was pinging from Cambria... "I hope you got to bust your nut because that's the last time you'll be getting anymore dick from him..." he laughed as he turned on the television...

"Hey Kenya..." Kevin greeted as he tried to kiss her...

"Uh uh – get your ass in the shower – Don't fuckin' touch me!"

"What the hell is wrong with you?! You never speak to me like that!"

"Get your ass in the shower – I'll see you when you get out – matter of fact – take your clothes off..."

"I'm not doing a damn thing until you tell me what the fuck is wrong with you..."

"This is what's wrong with me!!" she gritted as she shoved her phone in his face...

"Where did you get that?!"

"That's your response?! Are you fuckin' serious right now?!" Kevin didn't answer her. He stripped out of his clothes and stood there in front of her. Kenya looked him up and down and then she noticed the bracelet... "Did she give that to you?"

"Yes..."

"Take it off!!" Kevin took off the bracelet and handed it to her... "Pick up your clothes and give them to me..." Kevin did as he was told...

"Where are you going?" he asked as she headed towards the door...

"I'm going to the incinerator – get your ass in the shower – I'll be right back..." she answered on her way out the door as she slammed it...

"How the fuck did this happen?" he sighed as he went to get in the shower...

"What did I tell you?!"

"Baby – I can explain..."

"What did I tell you?!"

"You told me don't bring you any drama..." Kevin sighed...

"Who the fuck is Darnell Tompkins?!"

"What's Darnell got to do with this?!"

"I'm asking the questions muthafucka!!" she gritted as she walked over to him and back-slapped him so hard he fell back against the wall...

"Kenya – I love you – but don't ever do that again..."

"Or what?!" she gritted as she stood in his face with her hands on her hips...

51

"Baby... I know you're upset..." he said as he put his hands on her shoulders... "But you need to calm down – I can explain everything... but I need you to calm down... please..."

"What's to explain?! I already know you've been fuckin' Dana!"

"Yes..."

"Why Kevin?! Of all the women you could choose – why her?!"

"Because I could..."

"What the fuck is that supposed to mean?!"

"It means I'm a fucking idiot..." he sighed as he sat down on the bed and put his head in his hands...

"Who the fuck is Darnell?!"

"Darnell is her husband..."

"WHAT?!"

"How did you get the picture?"

"He sent it to me!"

"He sent it to you?! When?!"

"Right before I called you to come home..."

"Muthafucka!!"

"That makes two of you..."

"When you called me... I saw him..."

"You saw him?! Where?!"

"At the hotel..."

"Are you fuckin' kidding me?!"

"Kenya... I'm sorry..."

"What if he decides to blackmail you?!"

"I'll pay him..."

"You'll pay him?! For how long?! What if he doesn't want money?! What if he takes the pictures and goes to the County Executive?! We could wind up losing everything!! Out of all the women in the world – why'd you have to fuck her?!" she yelled as she broke down crying. Kevin put his arms around her and tried to console her...

"Baby – I'm sorry..."

"Let go of me!!"

"No!!" he snapped as he started crying...

"You promise me you'd never bring me any drama – how am I supposed to show my face around the office when I come to see you – oh my God – does anybody else know what's going on between you and Dana?!"

"Victoria knows..."

"I swear – I wish I never married your ass!!

"Please don't say that Kenya – I'm sorry..."

"You're only sorry 'cause you got caught..."

"No Baby – that's not true – I never wanted any of this to happen – I told Dana her husband knew – I just didn't think..."

"What the fuck did you just say?!"

"I told Dana her husband knew she was having an affair..."

"So – you thought her husband knew she was cheating – and it never dawned on you to end it?!"

"I underestimated him..."

"Let go of me Kevin..."

"Please don't leave me Kenya..." he pleaded as he held her tighter...

"I said let go of me..."

"Promise me you won't leave me..."

"I'm not promising you shit – now let go of me!!" Kevin reluctantly let go of her and she got up off the bed. Kevin got up off the bed and followed her into the kitchen and sat at the island. Kenya opened the cabinet, took two glasses out the cabinet, and set them down on the counter. Kevin watched as she took the bottle of Hennessey off the shelf and waited for her to pour them both a drink. Kenya sat the bottle on the counter and then she spoke... "Drink..." Kevin picked up his glass and drank the Hennessey down in one gulp. Kenya did the same and then she spoke again..."When did you suspect that Darnell knew about her affair?"

"I told Dana a man always knows..."

"Wait a minute – you actually talked about this?!"

"Yes..."

"When?!"

"This afternoon..."

"Tell me..." Kenya commanded as she poured them both another drink...

"Dana told me she wished we could be together..." Kevin sighed...

"She's in love with you?!"

"Yes..."

"What did you say?!"

"I told her I thought it was better if things stayed the way they are..."

"Bitch actually thought she had a chance!" Kenya laughed...

"I also told her you knew who I was before we got married..."

"That was none of her fucking business!!" Kenya exclaimed as she poured them another drink...

"I told her that to make it clear to her that I would never leave you for her..."

"You should've ended things with her a long time ago..."

"She told me she could never agree to me being with another woman..."

"Oh wow – this Bitch has the nerve to tell you what she won't put up with but meanwhile she expects her husband to put up with her cheating on him..."

"That's what I said..."

"Wait – What?!"

"I told her she expects her husband to put up with what she's doing and she said it was different because he didn't know..."

"So that's when you told her he knows – and then you took her to the hotel and fucked her – you are a piece of work!" she laughed as she poured them both another drink...

"I'm sorry..."

"Now that Darnell made sure we all know – you know what you have to do – right?!"

"It's over..."

"It better be..."

"It is – I'll never see her again – I promise..."

"Is there anybody else I need to know about?"

"No..." Kenya finished her drink, waited for Kevin to finish his drink, and then she spoke again...

"Do you love her?" Kevin didn't' answer her. He got up from the chair, went over to her, picked her up in his arms, and carried her to the bedroom....

"Oh my God – I need cofffeeeee!!!" I sighed as I rolled out of bed... "Shit – it's 4 o'clock – I need to get dressed!" Thank God I showered before I went to bed or I would've been up at 3 instead of 4. It didn't take me long to get dressed so at 4:15 I was ready to call my Uber... "Good – I'll be at the airport a little after 5 – that'll work..." I said as I hurried out the door...

"Good morning!" Darnell exclaimed as he jumped up out of bed. Darnell looked at his dick and smiled to himself as he grabbed it in his hand... "Don't worry D – as soon as we touch down I'm gonna take care of both of us..." he said as he walked to the bathroom. Darnell close his eyes and imagined a young woman sucking his dick as he peed... "Aaahhh..." he moaned as he

finished... "Time to make our dreams come true!"
he exclaimed as he went to get dressed... "4:15 –
let me get the Uber right now..." he said as he
took out his phone, ordered the Uber, and went
downstairs...

"Good morning..." I greeted as I got in...
"Chelle?"
"Yes..."
"You're going to the airport?"
"Yes..."
"Okay – let's go..."

"Shit!" Darnell exclaimed as he looked at
his phone... "Who the fuck cancels an Uber after
15 minutes! Muthafuckas!" Darnell picked up
his head and looked around in frustration and
panic... "I'll never get a taxi at this hour – what
am I gonna do? Oh shit – an Uber!" he exclaimed
as he ran out in front of the Uber before the light
turned green and started tapping on the window.
The driver let the window down on the passenger
side...

"Sir – I can't..."
"Please – I have to make a 6 a.m. flight –
my driver just cancelled on me after 15
minutes..."
"I'm sorry – I can't..."
"Wait a minute..." I said...
"Yes Maam?"
"Are you going to White Plains Airport?"

"Yes!" Darnell exclaimed...

"So am I – get in..."

"Um – I can't do that Maam..."

"I'll give you $100!!" Darnell exclaimed as he opened the door, got in the car, and closed it...

"Shit – fine with me – let's go!" the driver exclaimed as he sped off...

"I'm Darnell..." he said as he extended his hand. I was so mesmerized by his smile I didn't say anything... "This is the part where you tell me your name..."

"Oh... sorry..." I laughed... "I'm Chelle..."

"Pleased to meet you Chelle..." he breathed as he took my hand and kissed it. Feeling his breath on my hand sent a shiver down my spine and tingles to my clit... "Nice meeting you too..." I sighed as I took my hand away from him...

"Um – excuse me – you said something about $100..." the driver said as he pulled up in front of the entrance to the airport...

"Thank you..." Darnell said as he reached inside his top coat pocket, pulled out his wallet, took out $100, and handed it to the driver...

"You're welcome – and thank you!"

"Here..." he said as he handed me $40..."

"Umm... this is too much..."

"I want to reimburse you for your ride... and give you something extra for your kindness..." he said as he got out the car before I could object. Just as I was about to open the door, he opened the door for me... "C'mon..." he said as he extended his hand...

"Thank you..."

"Where's your bag?"

"In the trunk..." I answered as the driver opened the trunk. Darnell took my bag out the trunk and took me by the hand before I could object... "Darnell —you don't have to do this – I'm fine..."

"I don't recall giving you a choice..." he laughed as he pulled me towards the entrance along with our bags. When we got inside the airport I just stood there... "C'mon!" he laughed...

"No..."

"Okay... here's your bag..." he sighed as he moved my bag towards me...

"That's better..." I said as I took my bag in one hand and his hand with the other. Darnell beamed from ear to ear as we held hands walking through the airport...

"Let's use that kiosk over there to check in..." he said as he pointed at the kiosk...

"You use that one – I'll use this one..." I said as I let go of his hand...

"Okay..." he sighed. I could've used the same kiosk he was using but I wanted some privacy. We were both done at the same time... "C'mon..." he said as he took my hand again and we started walking towards Boeing 717....

"Where are you going?" I asked...

"We're going to the gate..."

"That's not what I mean..."

"Oh – you wanna know where I'm going!" he laughed...

"Yea..."

"I'm going to Bermuda..."

"Wow..."

"May I ask where you're going?"

"Yes..."

"Well?"

"Well what?" I laughed...

"Where are you going?!" he laughed...

"I'm going to Bermuda too..."

"Wow! Where are you staying?!"

"I'm staying at the Radisson Granada Beach Resort..."

"So am I..." he said as he smiled at me mischievously...

"So... are you meeting anyone?"

"No... You?"

"No..."

"If you were my lady – I wouldn't let you out of my sight..."

"If I were your lady – I wouldn't want to be out of your sight..."

"Are you serious?!"

"Are you really that surprised?"

"Well... if I'm being honest... yes..."

"Why are you so surprised? You're a gentleman, you know how to treat a lady, and you're easy on the eyes..." Darnell started to get emotional and it startled me... "I'm sorry – I didn't mean to make you uncomfortable..."

"It's not you..." he said as he dabbed his eyes... "Wait – actually – it is you..." he sighed as we sat down. I wasn't sure what to do so I sat beside him... "Why are you going to Bermuda by yourself?"

"Don't do that..."

"What?"

"Don't act like I didn't hear what you just said..."

"You first..."

"I'm going to Bermuda by myself because I want to..."

"That's it?"

"What's that supposed to mean?"

"No breakup? No girlfriends?"

"Typical..." I sighed as I shook my head....

"I'm sorry... I just thought..."

"You thought since I wasn't meeting anyone I must be meeting up with friends..."

"Well... yea..."

"Not that it's any of your business – but I'm going to Bermuda to relax on the beach, eat exotic food, drink as much as I want, and do whatever and whoever I want to do until next year..."

"Did you say whoever?!"

"I said whoever..." Darnell smiled at me again and I had to cross my legs as I began to squirt a little... "Now – about what you said..."

"My reasons for going to Bermuda by myself are the same as yours..."

"Don't do that..."

"Okay..."

"Why'd you get so emotional back there?" I asked as I took his hand...

"It's been a long time since a beautiful woman saw me the way you do..."

"Stop it..."

"I'm serious..."

"I'm sorry..." I noticed the expression on his face change and I became concerned... "You wanna talk about it?"

"Not really..."

"It's okay – we don't have to – you want some coffee?"

"I'd love some..."

"Okay – I'll go get us some..." I said as I got up and went over to Starbucks...

"Welcome to Starbucks – what can I get you?"

"I'll take two small caramel machiattos..."

"Okay – that'll be $10.08..." I gave her my card, paid for the coffee, put it back in my pocket, and turned to look back at Darnell. He smiled and waved before I turned back around...

"Is that your husband?" the cashier asked...

"No – we just met..."

"That's your husband..."

"No he's not – we just met..."

"I'm telling you – that's your husband..." she said as the barista put our coffees on the counter...

"How could you know that?"

"Remember – I told you first..."

"Are you serious?"

"I saw him propose to you..."

"What?!"

"I'm a sensitive – I see things sometimes..." I picked up our coffee and headed back over to Darnell...

"Here..."

"Thank you..."

"I hope you like it..."

"I like it whether I like it or not..." he said before taking a sip...

"That doesn't make any sense!" I laughed...

"I like it because you offered to buy me a cup of coffee..."

"You're welcome..."

"She broke my heart..." he sighed...

"I know..."

"How'd you know?"

"I felt it..."

"I went to Kay Jewelers yesterday to buy her a $5k tennis bracelet she wanted and Cindy told me someone just bought it..."

"Oh my God..." I whispered... "It was me..." Darnell smiled and I was confused... "Why are you smiling?"

"I'm smiling because I told my wife that someone that was more deserving than she was bought the bracelet..."

"Your wife?! You're married?!"

"Not for long..."

"What's that supposed to mean?!"

"I wrote a letter to my wife yesterday. I told her a lot of things in that letter. In my last paragraph I told her to do us both a favor and sign the divorce papers..."

"You asked your wife for a divorce in a letter?! So you're here because you can't face her?! Wow!!"

"It's not like that..."

"What's it like then?!"

"You're upset..."

"Of course I'm upset!! I'd be mortified if my husband did that to me!!"

"And I'm sure your husband would be mortified if you did to him what my wife did to me..." he sighed...

"I'm sorry — I shouldn't jumped the gun like that..."

"You're a woman — that's what women do — you defend each other — that's not something you need to apologize for..."

"What happened at Kay Jewelers?"

"I feel better knowing you got the bracelet..."

"Don't do that..."

"Okay. After Cindy told me someone bought the bracelet I picked out another one..."

"Oh wow..."

"It's beautiful..."

"I bet it's rose gold..."

"How'd you know?"

"I looked at that one too..."

"So... my phone rang... I answered it... it was my attorney... and..." Darnell started getting emotional again and I took his hand...

"It's okay – you don't have to tell me..."

"I want to tell you..."

"Okay..."

"He sent me a picture..."

"Oh Darnell! I'm so sorry!" Darnell pulled me into a kiss so fast it startled me... "Stop..."

"I'm sorry – I can't believe I just did that..."

"Is that why you asked your wife for a divorce?"

"I didn't ask for shit – I told her to do us both a favor and sign the divorce papers – and I also told her if she could file them while I'm away that'd be great..."

"Damn – she really broke your heart..."

"I suspected she was seeing someone for a while – I could've forgiven her if it was anyone else..."

"Oh my God! You know him?!"

"I know them both..."

"Both?! He's married too?!"

"He may not be married after his wife gets her Christmas gift from me..."

"Oh my God! You sent the picture to his wife?!"

"I sure did – you must think I'm awful..."

"I think what happened to you is awful – fuckin' Bitch – fuck her – and fuck him too – I'm glad you sent the picture – that's what the fuck he gets for fuckin' your wife – oh my God – now I wanna smack a Bitch!"

"I think I love you!" Darnell laughed...

"I'm sorry – I would never – they both knew what they were doing!"

"And now they can both have each other..." Darnell said as he smiled at me. Between his smile and that kiss, I was ready to go rub one out in the ladies room...

"Flight 1691 now boarding..."

"That's our flight..." he said as he jumped up and pulled me up out the seat...

"Okay!" I laughed as I grabbed my bag and he pulled me over to the gate...

"Wait here – I'll be right back..."he said as he hurried over to the flight desk... "Do you have any seats available in first class?" he asked, out of breath...

"Sir – there's a line..."

"I'm sorry – I'm trying to surprise my girlfriend over there..." he said as he pointed towards me and I waved...

"What can I do for you?"

"I want to upgrade our tickets to first class..."

"Okay – what's her name?"

"I don't know her last name..."

"I thought that was your girlfriend?" someone asked behind him...

"We just met..." Darnell answered...

"Aww... that's beautiful – let him go ahead – I love Christmas!" another woman exclaimed...

"Okay – we have two seats left – but I need her ticket..."

"Chelle – could you come 'ere?!"

"I'm coming!" I answered as I hurried over to the desk...

"Good morning Chelle – I need to see your ticket please..." the lady behind the desk said...

"Is something wrong?"

"Nothing we can't fix..." she answered as she began typing in the computer. I was beginning to wonder why so many people were staring at us... "Here you go – Merry Christmas!" she exclaimed as she handed us our tickets...

"First Class?! Wow!!"

"Merry Christmas!!" everyone exclaimed as they whistled and applauded. Darnell pulled me into his arms and kissed me as they all continued whistling and applauding...

"Let's get you on the plane..." the lady behind the desk said as she removed the rope so we could board...

"I can't believe you did that!" I exclaimed as I sat down...

"You're welcome..."

"You didn't have too – I would've been happy in coach..."

"I would've been happy in coach too – but now that I've met you – I'm happy I'm here..." he breathed as he kissed me again...

"Darnell... stop..."

"You don't want me to kiss you?"

"You're married – what if somebody sees us?"

"Who the fuck – you know what – I don't give a damn who sees us..." he breathed as he pulled me into a kiss and kissed me hard...

"Gotcha!" Ron said as he took the picture...

"Darnell? Darnell – where are you?!" Dana called out as she came inside and closed the door... "Darnell? Where is he?" she asked as she walked into the office... "Oh no..." she whispered as soon as she saw his ring on top of the pad next to the pen. Dana went to sit down at the desk and began to cry when she saw the picture... "Darnell... I'm sorry..." she whispered as she continued crying. She looked at the divorce papers and cried even harder... "Oh Darnell... we could've worked this out... I'm sorry..." Dana wiped her eyes, moved his ring to the side, moved the pen, picked up the pad, and began reading the letter he wrote...

"Yes Darnell... You did love me... You really love me... and I ruined it..."

"Oh my God – he was watching us – did he send any more pictures?!"

"I was fucking Kevin while you were buying me a Christmas gift – How could I be so stupid?!"

"You're already buying an engagement ring and wedding band for someone else?! How could you do that when we're still married?! I thought I meant something to you!!"

"You think I'm signing these divorce papers without a fight?! And you have the nerve to ask me to file them for you?! Guess again muthafucka – I'm not signing shit!! You want a divorce – you face me like a man and tell me you want a divorce – you don't leave me – nobody leaves Dana!!" Dana got up from the desk, went into the bedroom, and sat down on the bed. Before she could call Kevin, a text popped up from him...

"Dana,

It's over between us. Your husband sent my wife a picture of us in front of the hotel and she went ballistic. If I had known this when I saw him at the hotel yesterday I would've knocked the shit out of him because that's a bitch-ass move – he should've been man enough to confront me when he saw me but instead – he told me to tell my wife he said hello.

I know this isn't your fault and I'm not blaming you at all – I blame myself because it's my fault. I never should've started seeing you in the first place – especially because we work together – but I was weak when it came to you and instead of using logic and common sense, I let my other head lead me into trouble.

I'm going to spend every waking moment trying to make this up to my wife. She deserves better and I'm praying she can forgive me. I suggest you try and work things out with your husband if you can.

Kevin"

"Oh God... Please... No..." she cried as she stood up. Dana wiped her face and began taking off her clothes... "I'll deal with this on Tuesday – in the meantime – I'm going to take a shower –

make myself a mimosa – and maybe I'll get on the train and treat myself to a gift from Tiffany's – diamonds are a girl's best friend – and I need a friend right now..." she said as she went into the bathroom and turned on the shower. Dana stepped under the water, slid down to the drain, and cried as the water beat down on her. After about 15 minutes, she gave herself a pep talk... "C'mon dana – get it together..." she said as she stood up. Dana began to wash and condition her hair as she continued with her pep talk... "You have your whole life ahead of you – you're getting ready to retire, you'll collect a nice pension, and your husband doesn't want anything from you so you'll be living your best life!! Yaasss!!" she exclaimed as she rinsed out her hair and began washing her body... "Feel those titties? Yasss girl – you don't need a breast lift or silicone – you're fabulous! And you have good pussy! Kevin told you in the text he was weak when it came to you 'cause that's what the fuck you do! You make 'em weak!" Dana turned off the shower, stepped out, and walked in front of the mirror... "Pretty Bitch!" she exclaimed as she picked up the blow dryer, turned it on, and began to dry her hair...

"You never answered my question..." Kenya said as Kevin walked into the kitchen...
"I thought I did..." he said as he sat down at the table...

"Laying the pipe down the way you did doesn't answer my question – it does the opposite..."

"I'm sorry..."

"That doesn't answer my question either..." she said as she put two plates of scrambled eggs with cheddar, turkey sausage, potatoes with onions, and a crescent roll on the table. Kevin watched her as she made them both a cup of coffee and then he waited for her to put them down on the table. When she sat down, he took her hands and held them...

"Yes..." he answered as he teared up...

"I know..."

"You know?"

"Of course I knew..."

'How'd you know?'

"That's not important..." she answered as she began drinking her coffee...

"I swear – I'll never do this to you again..." he said as he began drinking his coffee...

"Don't make me a promise you don't intend to keep Kevin..."

"Kenya..." he sighed as he took her hand... "I messed up... I never should've started a relationship with someone I work with – especially Dana..."

"What does especially Dana mean?"

"I should've known better than to start something with a woman that has a husband that knows us both – it's my fault he was able to send you that email..."

"Eat your breakfast..." Kevin began to eat his breakfast and he slid his phone over to her so she could read the text he sent to Dana. Dana was quiet as she read the text... "I forgive you... but it's going to take some time for me to get over this..."

"I understand..." They both finished their breakfast without speaking...

"Alright now! Let's go get you a new man!" Dana exclaimed as she looked at herself in the mirror. Dana turned to the left, turned to the right, picked up her phone, and took a selfie... "Yaasss!" she exclaimed as she posted the picture with the caption 'Feeling Festive!' Dana went into the kitchen, opened the refrigerator, took out the orange juice, and took out the bottle of champagne. She went over to the cabinet, took out a champagne flute, and put it on the quartz counter next to the blender... "Let's see – one part orange juice – one part champagne – and mix!" she exclaimed as she blended the mixture. When she was done, she put the orange juice back in the refrigerator along with the champagne, closed the door, and picked up the blender... "This looks so good!" she exclaimed as she poured herself a glass. Dana put the blender back down, reached for her pills, and opened the bottles... "I'll take you..." she said as she picked up a lithium tablet and swallowed it... "And now I'll take you..." she said as she picked up a Risperdal tablet and swallowed it. Dana put the caps back on the bottles, picked up her mimosa, and raised her glass...

"Merry Christmas and Happy New Year to me!" she exclaimed and then she gulped down her mimosa... "Shit – that was good – I'ma pour me another one!" she exclaimed as she took the lid off the blender and poured herself another one... "Merry Christmas and Happy New Year!" she exclaimed again as she raised her glass and spilled some on the floor... "Oh shit!" she laughed and then she gulped down the 2nd mimosa... "Wooo... I shouldn't've had them back to back – I forgot to eat something first... tee hee hee... le'me sit down before I fall down..." she mumbled as she went to take a step, slipped in what she spilled, hit her head on the edge of the quartz countertop on the island, fell to the floor, and died instantly as the blood pooled beneath her...

"Ooohhh - let's go over there!" I exclaimed when I saw Einstein Bros. Bagels...

"You've been there before?"

"No – but they have good reviews – and I'm hungry..." I answered as I pulled him towards the restaurant...

"Good morning – what can I get you?"

"We'll look at the menu – take the next person in line..."Darnell answered...

"Next!" the casher called out as we looked at the menu...

"I want the turkey sausage & cheddar – with two eggs..." I said....

"I'll get the Applewood bacon & cheddar – with two eggs..." Darnell said...

"That sounds good too..."

"I'll give you half of mine and I'll take half of yours..."

"Okay!" I exclaimed...

"How do you want your coffee?" the cashier interrupted...

"Two caramel macchiatos..." Darnell answered as he pulled me close to him and held me around my waist...

"You got it..." the cashier confirmed...

"Can we sit down?" I asked...

"Sure..." Darnell answered as he took me to a table. We sat down and just stared at each other until they called our number...

"Number 15!" Darnell jumped up to get our food and I smiled as I watched him go to the counter...

"Your husband is fine!" she said as she walked by my table...

"Thank you girl!" I exclaimed...

"Where'd you find him?"

"I met him in an Uber on the way to the airport..."

"What?!"

"Yes girl – we're on the same flight..."

"You just met?! And you're already claiming him?!"

"Yea..."

"Le'me get over to my gate and find my husband!" she exclaimed as she left...

"What was that about?" Darnell asked as he sat down with our food...

"Nothing..."

"Nothing?"

"Girl talk..." I answered as I opened my sandwich and started eating. Darnell didn't push me for an answer – he opened his sandwich, gave me half of his, he took half of mine, and we continued eating without speaking...

"Delta flight 584 now boarding at airbus A319..."

"What seat do you have?" I asked before I got up. Darnell looked at his ticket...

"I'm in row 10, seat A..."

"I'm in row 10, seat B..."

"Good – let's go..." he said as he stood up. I stood up, he took my hand, and we hurried over to the gate...

"Welcome to the Radisson Grenada Beach Resort – are you checking in?"

"Yes..." we both answered...

"Name please?"

"Robinson..."

"Tompkins..."

"Is the room in both names?"

"I'm sorry – you can check her in first..." Darnell said...

"Yes Sir..."

"I can take you over here..." the young lady flirted as she motioned for Darnell to come over near her. Darnell looked at me, looked back at her, and then waited...

"Go ahead honey – I'll meet you upstairs..." I said as I got my room key and went to the elevator...

"Is that your lady?" she asked...

"Yes..."

"Why do you have separate rooms?"

"I'd rather not answer that..."

"Here's your key – you're in Suite 315..."

"Thank you..." Darnell said as he took the key and hurried over to the elevator...

"There you are..." he breathed...

"Here I am..."

"What Suite are you in?"

"I'm in Suite 313..."

"I'm in Suite 315..." he said as the elevator doors opened and he pulled me inside. The doors closed and Darnell was all over me...

"Darnell... wait..." I panted as he ran his hands up and down my back...

"Okay... I'll wait..." Thank God the doors opened when they did... "C'mon..." he said as he took my hand and pulled me down the corridor...

"My room's right here..." I laughed...

"My room's right here..." he said as he opened the door, pulled me inside, and pushed the door closed... "Darnell... wait..."

"I don't want to..." he breathed as he kissed me... "And you don't want me to..."

"Darnell... Stop..."

"You really want me to stop?"

"Yes..."

"Okay..." he sighed...

"I want you to come to my room in 10 minutes..." I said as I hurried out the door...

"Whew – that was close!" I exclaimed as I threw my bag on the bed and opened it. I pulled out my orange thong bikini, put it on the bed, stripped out of my clothes, and put the bikini on... "I hope this looks as good as it feels..." I sighed as I looked in the full length mirror... "Yes – I look good!" I exclaimed. I hurried over to the bed and looked in my suitcase for my orange stilettos... "Yes!" I exclaimed as I put them on. I took my time walking over to the door and made sure I unlocked it. I left it cracked so Darnell could come in, stopped in front of the mirror to admire myself, and then I strolled over to the balcony. I opened the door, stepped out, and leaned over the railing, making sure Darnell would have a clear view of my ass as soon as he opened the door...

"Chelle? Can I come in?"

"Come in Darnell..." Darnell came in and I heard him close the door and lock it...

"Damn..." he sighed as he came up behind me. I continued to look out at the beach over the balcony as he ran his hands up my body. I gasped when he squeezed my breasts... "You're fuckin' beautiful..." he breathed in my ear. I was so turned on I could've cum on myself. I heard his belt hit the balcony and I knew what was coming next. Darnell held my waist with one hand, moved my thong over with the other, and eased his dick inside me....

"Ooohhh... Darnell..." I moaned. He moved his other hand to my waist and tortured me with long, slow strokes..... "Huh... Huh... Huh..." I could tell Darnell cared more about pleasing me in that moment because the way he'd been all over me earlier I expected him to start pounding me – but he didn't... "Huh... Huh... Huh..." Darnell held me steady as my legs began to tremble and I stopped him... "Darnell... Stop..." He eased himself out of me and it felt so good I was about to change my mind and tell him to fuck me but instead I went with my first mind and turned around to face him. I pulled him towards me, wrapped my arms around his neck, kissed him, and he lifted me up. He eased himself inside me again and I wrapped my legs around his waist as he started to carry me off the balcony... "Stay here..." I commanded. Darnell knew exactly what I wanted... "Huh... Darnell... Yeess... Don't stop... I'm cumming..."

"Uggh... Uggh... Uggh... Uggh..."

"Haa... Haa... Haa... Haa..." Darnell continued to stroke me as I rode my orgasm out and then he took me to the bed and fell down on top of me...

"UUGH!   UUGH!   UUGH!   UUGH! UUUGGGHHH!!'

"Dana? Dana you in there? I came to take you to lunch!" Helen exclaimed as she continued knocking on the door... "Le'me go see if she's in there..." she sighed as she went around the side of their house... "Dana! Oh my God! Noooo!" she screamed...

"911 – What's your emergency?"

"My neighbor's hurt!"

"What's wrong Maam?"

"She's in her house on the floor – there's blood – please – hurry!"

"What's your address Maam?"

"710 Davenport Avenue – Unit 2 – New Rochelle – Please hurry!"

"We're dispatching someone right now Maam..."

"Thank God you're here!" Helen exclaimed as she ran up to the officers. The paramedics pulled up right behind them...

"You said she's inside?"

"Yes – she's in there!"

"Is anyone with her?"

"No – her husband isn't there – I have a key though..."

"Could you let us in?"

"Hell yea!" she exclaimed as she opened the door...

"Guys – we have a body!" the 1st officer yelled. The paramedics rushed inside and saw Dana on the floor...

"Dana! Noooo!"

"We need you to wait over there Maam..." the paramedics said as they went over to check her body... "She doesn't have a pulse..." the 1st paramedic said...

"Dana!" Helen cried...

"Maam – please have a seat in the living room..." the 1st officer requested. Helen went to sit down. The 2nd officer took pictures before the paramedics took her body and put it in the body bag...

"Daaannaaaa!" Helen cried as they wheeled her body out the door...

"Sullivan – I'm going to look around..." the 1st officer said as he looked around. He went in the master bedroom and then he went in the office... "Sullivan – could you come in here a minute?"

"I'll be right there..." Officer Sullivan said as he got up. Helen got up too...

"Maam – Please wait here..."

"Okay..." she sniffed as she sat back down...

"Take a look at this..." Officer Nunn said as he pointed at the desk...

"Oh shit..." Officer Sullivan sighed as he saw the letter with Darnell's wedding band on it..."

"Take a look at this..."

"Oh shit – are those divorce papers?'

"Yea..."

"Damn – that's fucked up - "You think she committed suicide?"

"No – she slipped and hit her head on the counter – let's go back out in the living room – I'll take another look in the kitchen while you talk to the neighbor..."

"Okay..." Officer Sullivan agreed...

"I can't believe it..." Helen sighed as Officer Sullivan sat down beside her...

"What's your name Maam?"

"Helen Thompson..."

"Are you friends with her?"

"She was my best friend..." Helen answered as she started crying...

"Does she have any family?"

"Her husband..."

"What's her husband's name?"

"Darnell Tompkins..."

"Do you have any idea where he is?"

"No..."

"Thank God you had a key to her house..."

"She gave it to me in case of an emergency... But I never thought I'd have to use it..." she cried as Officer Sullivan comforted her......"

"Sullivan – I need you to take a look at this..."

"I'll be right there..." he said as he got up...

"Look at that..." Officer Nunn said as he pointed to the medication...

"Hmmm – lithium, Risperdal, and alcohol – that's a bad mix..."

"Exactly..."

"What's that on the floor?"

"That's her cell phone..."

"Let's bag that – I don't expect the coroner will find out there was any foul play but I wanna take that phone with us..."

"Got it..." Officer Nunn said as he put on a glove, picked up the phone, and put it in a plastic bag... "While you're at it – let's get those other papers too..."

"I'm on it!" Officer Nunn exclaimed as he hurried into the office to get the divorce papers and the letter. Officer Sullivan went to sit back down with Helen...

"I'm so very sorry for your loss..."

"I'm gonna miss her..."

"I guess we can go now..." he said as he got up...

"Okay..." Helen sighed. Officer Nunn followed out the door behind them and Helen made sure the door was locked before she went back to her house...

"Hey Sullivan – come take a look at this..." Officer Nunn said. Officer Sullivan got up and went over to Officer Nunn's desk...

"What's this?"

"It's a text from the man she was cheating on her husband with..."

"Damn – she got dumped by her husband and her man – and now she's dead... Sad..."

"Now I'll just put her husband's information in here so we can find him..." Officer Nunn said as he put Darnell's information into the computer... "Got him!"

"Where is he?" Officer Sullivan asked as he leaned over Officer Nunn's shoulder...

"He's in Bermuda..."

"Oh shit – he found out his wife was cheating so he went to Bermuda to get some Holiday Pussy!"

"Well – I guess the good news will be that he doesn't need to worry about a divorce..." Officer Nunn sighed...

"Damn – that's cold..."

"So is his wife's body..."

"When does he get back from Bermuda?"

"He'll be back on Tuesday, January 3rd, at 10:30 p.m...."

"What airport will he be arriving at?"

"White Plains..."

"We'll be there at 10 so we can be sure to meet him at the gate..." Officer Sullivan said as he wrote down the information...

"What the..." I said as I looked around the room. Darnell was lying beside me and my suitcase was on the floor. Some of my things were on the floor too... "Darnell..."

"Huh?"

"We need to get up..."

"Why?"

"Darnell..."

"Huh?"

"C'mon – let's get dressed – I want to go to the beach..."

"Okay..." he yawned. I got up off the bed, stood at the foot of it, put my hands on my hips, and looked at him. Darnell got up and I had a few moments to admire is naked body as he walked over to the balcony to get his clothes. He knew I was looking at him so he took his time getting dressed. I didn't start getting dressed until he was finished. I went towards the door and before I could open it, Darnell turned me around to face him and pulled me into a kiss... "Thank you..."

"For what?"

"For giving yourself to me..." I started tearing up... "What's wrong?"

"Nothing..." I answered as I smiled...

"You know you're mine now – right?"

"As long as you're mine... That's fine..." I sighed. Darnell opened the door and we went downstairs...

"Where would you like to go first?" he asked...

"Let's go to Esther's – it's a 5-minute walk from here..."

"Okay..."

"Welcome to Esther's – what can I get you?"

"I'd like a Screaming Orgasm..." I answered as everyone behind me laughed...

"My wife had a few screaming orgasms about an hour ago!" someone said and we all laughed..."

"I'll have an Adios Mother Fucker!" Darnell exclaimed as everyone laughed...

"I can't believe they actually have that on the menu!" I exclaimed...

"They do!" he exclaimed as I looked at the menu and began reading... "Let's see – Vodka, Gin, Tequila, Rum, Blue Curaçao, Lime Juice, & Sprite..." I read out loud...

"I hope you can carry him..." the gentleman laughed as he served us our drinks...

"I'll be fine..." Darnell laughed as we sat down...

"Would you like any snacks?" the server asked...

"No thank you..." I answered...

"Take your time – they're very generous with the alcohol..." Darnell warned as we started sipping. By the time we were finished, the sun was setting and we were hungry for more than snacks... "Let's go find something to eat..." he said as he stood up...

"Okay..."I said as I stood up and almost fell back down...

"Are you okay to walk?" he laughed...

"I think so..." I answered as I got up again...

"C'mon..." he laughed as he helped me up and we walked over to Carib Sushi...

"I don't know if there's anything I can eat..."

"You don't eat raw fish?"

"No..."

"C'mon – I'm sure we'll find something..." he said as we went inside...

"Table for two?"

"Yes..." Darnell answered...

"Right this way..." We followed the gentleman to the table and sat down. The menus were already on the table so we didn't have to wait...

"Oh my God – this is expensive!" I exclaimed...

"Don't worry about that – order whatever you want..."

"Welcome to Carib Sushi – may I take your order?" the server asked...

"I'll have the Pink Shrimp..." I answered...

"And you Sir?"

"I'll have the Long Island Strip – well done..."

"And for dessert?"

"I'll have the vanilla ice cream..."

"I'll have the chocolate ice-cream..."

"I'll be back with your Prosecco..." the server said as he went to place our order...

"I don't want anything else to drink..." I said...

"Wait until you eat something – you'll feel better..." The server brought our soup and salad to the table and walked away again...

"This onion soup is good..." I sighed...

"Feeling better?"

"Yea..." I finished the soup and started on the salad... "The ginger sauce is a little spicy – but I like it..."

"How'd you know it was ginger sauce?"

"I've had it before..." I answered as we finished our salad...

"Here you are..." the server said as he put our main course on the table...

"Oh my God! Look at these shrimp! They're so big!"

"This strip looks delicious..." Darnell sighed as he cut into it and took a bite...

"How is it?"

"Mmm..." he moaned as he licked his lips. I had to turn away from him because I started blushing... "How's your food?"

"It's delicious..." Darnell knew what he was doing and he smiled at me. We didn't say anything else as we ate...

"Here's your dessert..." the server said as he put the chocolate ice-cream in front of Darnell and the vanilla ice-cream in front of me. When he took our plates, Darnell put some ice cream on his spoon and he was deliberately showing me what he wanted to do to me with his tongue once we got back upstairs. We finished our ice cream, he paid the check and we took our time walking along the beach back to our hotel in the moonlight...

"Well... I guess I'll call it an early night... Thank you for a lovely evening..." I sighed as we got to Darnell's door...

"You got jokes..." he laughed as he opened the door and pulled me inside...

"Darnell... I..." he interrupted me by kissing me. I continued to stand there as he went to the bed and pulled back the covers and sheets. I watched him get undressed and then he came over to me, took me by the hand, and led me over to the bed. I didn't say anything as he undressed me. When I was completely naked, he spoke...

"Get on your back..." I got in the bed and did what I was told. Darnell got on the bed on his knees, and got on top of me...

"Darnell..." I whispered. He kissed me from my neck, down my body to my pelvis, and then he stopped. My pussy was dripping in anticipation as he picked up my legs, spread them, and moved his head down between them... "Oh Darnell!" I moaned as he began to do everything he did to that spoon in the restaurant... "Darnell... Oh God... Yesss..." His tongue was like nothing I've ever felt because this was my first time ever experiencing this... "Oh Darnell... Huh...." He continued to flick, lick, suck, and slurp and my eyes rolled in back of my head as I arched my back... "I'm cumming... I'm cumming..." My legs began to tremble and when my body shook I was startled...

"Let it go..." he whispered...

"Haa... Haa... Haa... Haa... HHHAAA!!" Darnell came up from between my legs, kissed me, and I knew he knew...

"I was your first..."
"Yea..."

"I have something for you..." he said as he got up. I sat up in the bed and watched him go in his suitcase and take out a gift-wrapped box... "Merry Christmas..." he said as he handed me the box. When I opened the box and saw the diamond tennis bracelet in rose gold, I cried...

"Oh Darnell – it's beautiful... but..."

"I know what you're thinking..."

"You do?"

"After I found out my wife cheated on me I told Cindy I still wanted to buy the bracelet because I wanted to give it to the woman that would be my Now & Forever..."

"Oh Darnell... I can't..."

"You already gave yourself to me... You're mine now..." he said as he took the bracelet and put it on my wrist... "And forever..."

"Oh Darnell..." I cried...

"Merry Christmas..." he breathed as he kissed me again and pushed me back down on my back...

"Good morning..." he breathed as he kissed me awake...

"Good morning..." I yawned...

"What would you like to do today?"

"I need to go back to my room..." I answered as I stretched...

"Can I come?"

"Yes..."

"Why are we going back to your room?"

"I want to put on another thong bikini and spend the day on the beach..."

"How long have you been an exhibitionist?"

"I'm not really an exhibitionist..."

"You wanted me last night... on the balcony... where you could be seen..."

"I spend my whole day being conservative – the only time I can be free and comfortable is when I get home – I couldn't wait to get here so I could do who I please, as I please, when I please, with whoever I please..."

"Thank you for doing as you please..." he breathed as he kissed me... "When you pleased..." he breathed as he kissed me again... "With me..."

"I need coffee..." I yawned...

"Is that all you need?" he breathed as he kissed me again...

"I need food..."

"Is that all you need?" he breathed as he kissed me again...

"I need you..."

"I need you too..." he breathed as he kissed me again... "But if I don't get out this bed right now... I won't get up at all..."

"Merry Christmas..." Kevin breathed as he kissed Kenya awake...

"Merry Christmas..." she yawned...

"I made breakfast..."

"Okay... I'm coming..."

"Not yet..." he said as he smiled at her mischievously. Kenya got out the bed, put on her robe, and went into the dining room...

"Oh Kevin..." she sighed. Kevin had the table decorated in red, green, and gold. Kenya went to the table and sat down in front of the plate with the gift box wrapped in red paper with a gold bow... "This... This is beautiful..." she sighed...

"Open it..."

"Can I wait until after I have my coffee?"

"No... Open it..."

"Okay..." she sighed. Kevin watched her intently as she took her time removing the wrapping paper...

"Will you hurry up!" he exclaimed as he laughed...

"Okay, okay..." she laughed as she removed the last bit of paper and opened the box... "Kevin..." she whispered as she started crying...

"Merry Christmas..." he said as he got up, took the diamond tennis rose quartz bracelet from her, and put it on her wrist...

"This is so beautiful... Thank you!" she breathed as she pulled him into a kiss...

"You're welcome - I'll be right back..." Kenya sat there admiring her bracelet as she turned her wrist back and forth. Kevin came back into the dining room with their coffee... "Thank you..." she sighed as she took a sip. Kevin went to get their plates and when he came back into the dining room, her eyes got really big... "French toast?"

"Yes..." Kenya got up from the table... "Where are you going?"

"I'll be right back..." she said as she went into the kitchen. Kevin laughed when she came back with her cell phone...

"Are you serious?!"

"I sure am!" she exclaimed as she took a picture of her plate and sat back down... "I need you to do me a favor..."

"Sure..."

"Open the top drawer to that china cabinet..."

"Okay..." Kevin opened the drawer and saw a small box wrapped in red paper with a blue bow on it... "Is this what you need?" he asked as he picked it up...

"Yes..." Kevin sat down at the table, unwrapped the box, and opened it...

"Oh my God..."

"Merry Christmas..." Kevin got up from the table, went over to Kenya, and pulled her up into his arms...

"I love you..." he breathed as he kissed her hard...

"You're welcome..." Kevin sat back down, took the ring out the box, and put it on his pinky. The diamond ½ ct round cut 10k two-toned white and rose gold was the perfect complement to the tennis bracelet he gave her... "Are you going to wear it?"

"Hell yea..." he sighed... they both finished their coffee and French toast without speaking. When they were finished, Kevin got up from the table and took the plates...

"Let me get that..." Kenya said...

"No – you go relax... I got it..."

"Okay..." she agreed as she got up, went into the living room, and sat on the couch. Kenya turned on the Christmas lights and watched them as she listened to Kevin in the kitchen.

When he came into the living room and sat down with her, she spoke... "I'm curious..."

"About what?"

"Please don't be mad..."

"Why would I be mad?"

"Because I want to ask you something..."

"You want to know what I bought Dana for Christmas..." he sighed...

"How did you know that's what I was going to ask you?"

"Because I know you..."

"So what did you get her?"

"Well..."

"That nice huh?"

"She collects Disney Villains..." Kenya bust out laughing... "You know where I'm going with this huh?" he laughed...

"I bet I do!" she laughed...

"I bought her the Disney Evil Queen boxed set..."

"I knew it!" she exclaimed as they both bust out laughing...

"Thank you..." I sighed as we finished breakfast...

"You're welcome..."

"Let's go back to my room..."

"I need to take a shower..."

"You can take a shower in my room... with me..."

"All my things are here..."

"You can bring them to my room..."

"I guess I can do that..." he said as he went to get swimming trunks out his suit case. I waited for him to get his razor, deodorant, shaving cream, and toothbrush and then we went to my room...

"Come with me..." he said as he pulled me into the bathroom. He turned on the water, stepped into the shower, and pulled me inside...

"It's cold!" I shrieked...

"It'll warm up in a minute..." he breathed as he pushed me back against the wall. I wrapped my arms around his neck and braced myself as he lifted me up and I wrapped my legs around his back...

"Oh... Darnell... Huh..." I moaned as the water beat down on us. He was deep inside me and I locked my ankles around his back...

"Uggh... Uggh... Uggh..." Darnell... Huh... Darnell..." I held on tighter as he fucked me harder... "Uggh! Uggh! Uggh! Uggh!"

"Darnell... I'm cumming... I'm cumming... Haaaahhh..."

"Uuugh! Uuugh! Uuugh! Uuugh! UUUGGGHHH!!" We started kissing profusely as the water beat down on us and I unlocked my ankles... "Damn..." he breathed as he helped me stand up... I stood still as he lathered up the loofah with body wash and washed me. When he was done, I lathered up the loofah, washed him, and we got out the shower... "I'm going to shave right quick..."

"Mmm Hmm..." I mumbled as I brushed my teeth. I left him in the bathroom and went to dry off. I was dressed when he came out. Darnell caught me looking at his dick and he smiled...

"Stop that..."

"What am I doing?" he asked as he smiled at me mischievously...

"You're making me want to change my mind..." I answered as I walked over to him and took his dick in my hand...

"Don't start..."

"You're the one that started it..." I said as I stroked his dick...

"Okay – that's it!" he growled as he threw me down on the bed...

"Darnell – wait!" I exclaimed...

"Why?!"

"It'll be worth it – trust me..."

"Okay..." he sighed as he got up. Darnell put his boxers on, I picked up our phones, put them in my purse, I put the strap across my shoulder, and we left to go down to the beach...

"It sure is beautiful here..." I sighed as I went into the water...

"It sure is – Can you swim?"

"Yes..."

"Come with me..." he said as he took my hand and we went deeper...

"Let's go over there behind the rocks..." I whispered...

"Okay..." he agreed as he smiled at me mischievously. When we got over there, we caught another couple fucking...

"Oh my God!" she exclaimed...

"Don't mind us..." I said as I took out my phone...

"Are you fucking kidding me?! You're taking pictures?!"

"I'm not taking pictures of you..." I answered... "I want you to take pictures of us..."

"WHAT?!" Darnell exclaimed along with her Bae...

"Here..." I said as I handed her my phone. They all smiled as I posed in front of Darnell and put his hands around my back. My new friend understood the assignment as we began kissing...

"Oh yes... Sexy!" her Bae exclaimed. Darnell was shocked when I turned myself around towards the rocks, braced myself, and let the water support my body as I pulled him down on top of me...

"Are you sure about this?" I answered his question by pushing his trunks down over his ass and locking my ankles behind his back...

"Hell yea! Give it to her good!" her Bae exclaimed as she continued taking pictures.

Happy New Year

Darnell pushed his tongue in my mouth as he fucked me in the water...

"Mmmph...   Mmmph...   Mmmph... Mmmph... MMMMPPPPHHH!!" We continued kissing as a few other couples applauded...

"Damn that was hot!" I heard someone say...

"Thank you..." I breathed as I held out my hand and she gave me my phone...

"Oh no – thank you!" she exclaimed...

"Damn Babe – We should've brought our phone too!" her Bae exclaimed as I put my phone in my purse...

"Was it worth is?" I asked...

"Hell yea!" Darnell breathed as he pulled me into a kiss...

"Have a nice day!" she exclaimed as she took her Bae's hand and they swam away along with the other couples...

"Have you ever done that before?"

"No..."

"Have you always wanted to do that?"

"Not always..."

"I want a copy..."

"I know..." I said as I sat down on the rocks and took out my phone. Darnell watched as I forwarded him the pictures. I picked two pictures and forwarded them to Veronica...

"Oh shit!!" she exclaimed as she looked at the pictures and realized I was in Bermuda with Dana's husband...

"I really need some coffee..." I sighed...

"C'mon – Let's go to Le Papillion French Creole Café – they do breakfast and lunch..." Darnell suggested...

"Fine with me..." I agreed as Darnell took my hand and we walked to the Café...

"Welcome to Le Papillion – can I start you off with something to drink?" the waitress asked...

"Coffee – Please!" I exclaimed...

"We have cappuccino – is that alright?"

"Yes – Thank you!"

"I'll have the same..." Darnell said...

"I'll be right back..."

"I can't wait to eat – everything looks so good!" I exclaimed as I looked over the menu..."

"It does look good..." Darnell agreed...

"Here's your coffee..." the waitress said as she put our cups on the table...

"Thank you!" I exclaimed as I picked up my spoon and began sipping with it...

"Are you ready to order?"

"I'll have Eggs En Cocotte: eggs, sautéed potatoes, toast, & bacon..." I answered...

"Okay – how 'bout you sir?"

"I'll have the Spiced French Toast dipped in cinnamon sugar, topped with sautéed apples, candied walnuts, & passion fruit fromage cream..."

"I'll be back with your breakfast..." she said as she walked away and I finished my cappuccino...

"You really needed that coffee – huh?" Darnell laughed...

"Yeeesss..." I sighed. Darnell smiled at me as he sipped his coffee and just as he was finished, the waitress came back with our food...

"Oh my God – this looks delicious!" I exclaimed...

"Wait 'till you taste it..." she laughed as she walked away and we started eating...

After we left the restaurant we wanted to do some sight-seeing so we went to Tobacco Bay. The Bay was surrounded by stone that created a separation from the ocean and the waves.

Happy New Year

The rest of the week went by so fast. We continued to go sightseeing every day and went to the following places:

St. Peters Church, Fort St. Catherine, The Unfinished Church, Kings Square, The Globe Hotel Museum & Trustworthy Gift Shop, Achilles Bay Beach, Town Hall, Somers Garden, St. George's Visitor Information Center, Old Rectory, and The Dragon's Lair Gallery that had treasures from water color scenes by local artists and cedar boxes made from Bermuda cedar.

When we got hungry we had Grilled Ribeye Steak with garlic-scented mashed potatoes, sautéed onions, wilted greens, and Smokey Pineapple Chicken Breasts with cilantro rice & sautéed Swiss chard at Coconut Beach.

When we wanted appetizers we had Carriacou Love Bites (fish), Umbrellas Nachos, Umbrellas Wings, Pulled Pork Sliders, Grilled Chicken Tacos, and Crispy Fish Tacos at Umbrella's Beach Bar.

We had drinks at Esther's in the evenings, breakfast at Le Papillion on the days they were open, and we also made sure we stopped at Carib Sushi.

When we weren't sightseeing, we were drinking, and when we weren't drinking, we were fucking back and forth between my bed, his bed, my shower, and his shower. The only think we didn't do was another public display on the beach and every time a few of the couples that saw us spotted us, they reminded us by whistling, clapping, and applauding. Before we knew it, it was New Year's Eve...

"Good morning..." Darnell breathed as he kissed me awake...

"Good morning..." I yawned. I sat up, rubbed my eyes, and looked around...

"What's wrong?"

"I wasn't sure what room we were in..." I laughed...

"I can't believe how much we've been drinking..."

"We're gonna need a week to detox from alcohol!" I laughed...

"Naa..." he said as he shook his head back and forth... "You're the lightweight!"

"I need to go back to my room..."

"Why?"

"I ran out of clothes..."

"We'll go downtown later, after breakfast, and buy you some more..."

"It's going to be crazy in Kings Square – everyone will be shopping for tonight..."

"You're right – speaking of tonight – I was thinking..."

"Yes Darnell?"

"We can do Kings Square at 8 p.m. We can enjoy the entertainment and the food until 9:30 and then we can go to the New Year's Party on the yacht leaving from Dock 1 on Hamilton..."

"You mean to tell me you don't want to see the Bermuda Onion Drop?" I laughed...

"Actually – No..." he laughed... "I'd rather be on the yacht looking over the water, watching the fireworks, drinking champagne, dancing... and fucking you..." he answered as he smiled at me mischievously...

"How are you going to bring the New Year in fucking me if we're on a yacht?"

"You'll find out..."

"Okay – that's it..." I said as I got up out the bed...

"Where are you going?"

"I'm going to get in the shower – we have a busy day ahead of us..." I answered as I hurried into the bathroom and stepped in the shower...

"You didn't really think you were going to start without me... did you?"

"Nope!" I exclaimed as I turned on the water...

"Damn that's cold!"

"Now you know how it feels!" I laughed...

"You're gonna pay for that!" he said as he pulled me underneath the shower head...

After Darnell made sure I had my coffee and a good breakfast at Le Papillion, we went to Things We Love on Water Street...

"Oh Darnell... I love this store!"

"I knew you would..."

"Welcome to Things We Love – what can I help you with?" the associate asked...

"I see what I want..." I sighed...

"Take your time – I'm here when you're ready..." she said as she went back to the register and relaxed. Darnell stood back and watched me with her... "Is that your wife?"

"Not yet..." he answered as he smiled at me mischievously. I saw the associate smile and I knew they were having a conversation about me. I spent an hour looking at their eclectic bohemian fashion, picked out a few things, and went to the register...

"Did you forget anything?"

"Nope..."

"Okay – I'll take care of this for you..." she said as she rang it up and bagged it. Darnell came up behind me, gave her his card, and made sure I didn't see the receipt when she gave it to him... "Have a great day..." she said as we walked out...

When we got to Occasions Bridal & Formal I knew I wouldn't be in there long...

"Welcome to Occasions Bridal & Formal – My name is Ju – How can I help you?"

"I'm looking for a formal gown in pink..."

"Come with me..." she said as she took me over to the gowns...

"I want that one!" I exclaimed as I pointed to the Lovely Reese Cowl-Neck Convertible Maxi Slip Dress...

"Hmm – you look like you're about a size... 8 – here we are – go try it on and let me know what you think..." she said as she handed it to me...

"Darnell – could you hold these bags for me?" Darnell came over to get the bags...

"Would you like me to come help you?" Ju asked...

"Yes please..."

"Okay..."

"Well Darnell – what do you think?" I asked as I came out the dressing room...

"Wow..." he whispered as I turned around in front of the mirror...

"I guess you'll take it?" Ju asked...

"I'll take it..."

"Would you like to see our accessories?"

"Yes..."

"Come with me..." I followed her over to the shoes and saw exactly what I wanted...

"I'll take the Felicity Nude Touch Ups – size 7..."

"Okay – would you like anything else?"

"I'll take the Touch Ups Handbag..."

"Excellent..."Ju sighed... "Okay Sir – now that we're done with your wife – what can I do for you?" Darnell and I looked at each other and smiled...

"I need a tuxedo that will complement her dress..."

"I have just the suit for you..." she said as she picked up the Slim Shawl Collar Tuxedo – The Ethan By After Six – in black...

"That's the one – I'm..." Darnell started to say...

"I'll take your measurements..." Ju interrupted. Darnell stood still as she took his measurements and then she went to get the suit, shirt, socks, and a matte satin clip bowtie by After Six in carnation that was the perfect match to my dress... "Here you go – let me know if you need any help – if you do – I'll send your wife in there..."

"Okay..." Darnell laughed as he went in the dressing room. When he came out my jaw dropped... "You like what you see?" Darnell asked...

"Hell yea!" Ju and I both exclaimed and then we bust out laughing...

"Alrighty then!" Darnell laughed as he went back into the dressing room. When he came out, Ju hurried over to him...

"I'll get these..." she said as she took the items from him and hurried back to the counter... "You guys make a beautiful couple..." she said as she rang everything up...

"Thank you..." we both said. Ju handed the bags to Darnell...

"I'll take the other bags..." I said as I took two bags from him and we left...

Our last stop was Boyles Shoe Store and Darnell saw exactly what he was looking for...

"Excuse me... Sir..." the manager called out to him...

"I'll take these..." Darnell said as he picked up a pair of Brenston Minimalist Dress Shoes in black...

"What size would you like?"

"Size 9..."

"I'll see you at the register..." the manager said as he went to go get the shoes. We went to the register and we didn't have to wait long... "Here you are..." the manager said as he handed Darnell the bag...

"Here you are..." Darnell said as he handed the manager his card...

"Thank you – have a great day..." he said as we left the store and went straight back to the hotel...

"What room are we going to?" Darnell asked...

"Mine..." I answered as I opened the door. When we got inside Darnell didn't waste any time...

"Let's get in bed..."

"Okay..." I sighed as I stripped out of my clothes and got in the bed. Darnell stripped out of his clothes, got in bed with me, and we caught up on a few more hours of sleep...

"Darnell!" I exclaimed as I jumped up...

"Whh... What's wrong?!"

"We're gonna be late! We over-slept! We need..." Darnell interrupted me with a kiss...

"Stop..."

"Okay..."

"We're not going to be late..."

"But it's 8"00 – they started..." Darnell interrupted me with a kiss again... "Okay..." I sighed...

"We're not going to Kings Square..."

"We're not?"

"No..."

"So we're not going to be late..."

"No..."

"So... What are we going to do until 9:30?" I asked as I smiled at him mischievously...

"I'm sorry Chelle – I'd love to make love to you – but I need you to wait until we get on the boat..."

"I don't wanna fuck on the boat where everybody can see us – I don't wanna wind up on Instagram!" Darnell pulled me into another kiss and at this point I figured I might as well give up... "I know you don't wanna wait..." he breathed as he kissed me again... "But it'll be worth it..." he breathed as he kissed me again... "I promise..." he breathed as he kissed me one more time...

"Stop it!" I laughed as I pushed him away from me...

"Can't control yourself huh?" he laughed as he got up out the bed, grabbed his dick, and shook it at me...

"That's not fair!" I exclaimed as I jumped across the bed and tried to grab his dick but he jumped away just as I was about to reach it...

"Uh Uh Uh..." he teased...

"Darnell... Please?"

"Oohhh... You're begging... I like that..."

"Please Darnell..." I begged as I got up and went over towards him... "Please Darnell..." I begged as I began to run my hands on his body. Just when my hand got to his dick he stopped me...

"Soon..." he breathed as he moved my hand, turned his back, and walked into the bathroom. I followed him into the bathroom, stepped into the shower with him, and fought like hell to keep from touching him as he deliberately took his time lathering his body. I washed myself as quick as I could and when I went to step out the shower, he grabbed me... "Where do you think you're going?"

"I'm going to get dressed..."

"Stay and watch..." he commanded as he continued to torture me by lathering up his dick with his hands. I nearly lost it when he started massaging his balls and I began to touch myself... "Uh Uh Uh..." he laughed as he moved my hand away. He finally rinsed himself off, turned off the water, and allowed me to step out. I watched him step out and hurried to grab the towels so he couldn't wrap one around his body. He smiled at me as he strolled by, making sure to rub his dick on my ass as he passed me on his way out the bathroom. I decided right then and there that I didn't give a damn who was on that boat – I was going to make him pay...

"Are you ready?" he asked as if he didn't already know the answer...

"I'm ready..." We stood there admiring each other in the mirror and I took a bunch of selfies...

"Damn we look good..." he sighed. I went to get the bracelet he gave me for Christmas and stopped in front of the mirror again... "Let me help you..." he said as he put the bracelet on my wrist. We stopped to admire ourselves in the mirror again and this time I made sure to put my wrist up so it would show in the selfie. Darnell waited for me to put my phone away and then he took my hand and we headed out...

"Darnell look!" I exclaimed... "How did this line get so long already?!"

"Don't worry about it..."

"It's 10:00 – I'm not sure I can stand that long in these shoes!"

"I know that's right – my feet already hurtin' and I ain't even on the boat yet!" someone exclaimed from behind me...

"Attention everyone! We'll begin boarding shortly!"

"Oh thank God!" I exclaimed...

"Why do you wear heels if you can't stand in them?" Darnell laughed as I saw another yacht pull up...

"Oh shit – somebody booked a Bergen Yacht!"

"I wish we were on that!"

"Me too!"

"Come with me..." Darnell said as he took my hand and led me towards the Bergen Yacht...

"Oh Darnell..." I sighed as he led me on...

"Here you are Mr. Tompkins – I'll see you next year..." the captain said as he handed Darnell the keys. I watched the captain leave the boat and realized it was just the two of us...

"Darnell... You did this... for me?"

"I told you..." he breathed as he pulled me into a kiss... "I wanted to bring the New Year in eating..." he breathed as he kissed me... "Drinking..." he breathed as he kissed my neck... "And fucking you..." he breathed as he took my hand, put it on his dick, and began rubbing his dick with my hand...

"Oh Darnell..."

"Come with me..." he said as he took me by the hand and led me upstairs to the bridge...

"Darnell – you're driving?"

"I'm driving..." he answered as he escorted me to my seat and I sat down...

"This is beautiful..." I sighed as I relaxed in the comfort of the leather...

"You haven't seen anything yet..." he said as he sat in his seat, started the engine, and began to steer the boat...

The sun was setting and I took out my phone to take pictures of the purple, pink, and orange sky...

"Come with me..." Darnell said as he turned off the engine, got up, and extended his hand to take mine. I got up and he walked me around the boat. I took a few selfies of us on deck and then he took my hand again... "Come downstairs..." he commanded. I followed him downstairs and I was in awe...

"A lower deck..." I sighed. We sat in the chairs so I could take a few selfies and then he stopped me...

"Open the doors." I got up to open the doors and I was in awe...

"Oh Darnell!" I exclaimed as I stretched out on the leather couch...

"Not yet..." he said as he came over to me and helped me up. Darnell took me into the kitchen and I saw another steering wheel and control board...

"You can steer from down here too?"

"Yes..." he answered as he went over to the controls and turned on jazz... "Dance with me..." he commanded. He took a remote out his pocket, pushed it, and I saw us dancing on the flat screen...

"Oh Darnell..."

"Yes Chelle...' he breathed as he kissed me. We danced for a while and I managed to get a picture of us on the flat screen as he changed the music and That's What I Like by Bruno Mars, started playing. Darnell pulled me to him and we continued dancing as he began to sing to me and I cried. We didn't bother to stop dancing to get any tissues but it didn't matter because he kissed my eyes and my tears as they fell down my face. It was my turn when Fantasy Baby by Mariah Carey started to play and Darnell was mesmerized as I sang and danced. Just as I started thinking about making him pay I remembered we were on the flat screen...

"Is that recording?"

"Yes..." he answered as he led me into the private kitchen and stood me in front of the dishwasher...

"Darnell..." I started to say as he lifted my dress up...

"The camera can't see below the counter... be still..." he whispered in my ear as he slid my thong over... "Beg me..."

"Please Darnell..." I begged as he eased himself inside me...

"Again..."

"Please... Darnell..." I panted as he began stroking me. I looked at the flat screen and watched us as he continued stroking... "Huh... Darnell... Yes..." Darnell grabbed my hips and began stroking me harder... "Oh Darnell... I'm cumming..."

"Cum for me..."

"Aah... Aaah... Aaah... Aaah..."

"Uggh... Uggh... Uggh... Uggh..."

"What are you doing?" I laughed as he got down and went between my legs...

"I'm going in the fridge – be still..." he commanded. When he came back up from between my legs, he had a plate of fruit, meat, cheese, and crackers...

"Wow..."

"Wow indeed..." I looked at the flat screen again and I was happy the camera couldn't see what happened behind the counter. Darnell put the plate on the table and came back into the kitchen... "Why are you still standing here?"

"I don't know..." I laughed...

"Well – as long as you're standing there – could you get two champagne flutes out the cabinet?"

"I can't reach it..."

"Fine – I'll get the flutes – you get the champagne..." he said as he took the flutes down off the shelf... "C'mon..." he commanded. I followed him over to the couch and sat down as he poured champagne for us and picked up his glass... "Here's to us..."

"Here's to us..." I repeated and then we both sipped...

"Eat..." he commanded...

"This is so good..." I breathed as we ate and continued drinking. I went to pick up the bottle and he stopped me...

"Save some for later..."

"Okay..." I sighed. I sat back, relaxed, and took a few more pictures of us on the flat screen before he went back in the kitchen. I watched him take another plate out the refrigerator and I was in awe. I saw steak, shrimp, lobster, scallops, and mixed vegetables. Darnell took out another plate with bowtie pasta... "Where'd you get all that?" I asked as I went into the kitchen...

"I told them what I wanted when I booked it..." he answered as he took out the wok, turned on the flame, put some olive oil in the wok, and began cooking. I went to sit back down and took a few pictures of him cooking on the flat screen as well as in the kitchen...

"Chelle..." I didn't realize I dozed off...

"Yes Darnell..." I yawned...

"Dinner is ready..." he said as he put the plates on the table and poured two more glasses of champagne...

"Oohh... This looks good..." I sighed as we began to eat. We finished eating and Darnell raised his glass again...

"Here's to eating, drinking, and fucking on a yacht..."

"Here's to eating, drinking, and fucking on a yacht..." I repeated and then we both sipped. We continued drinking until the glasses were empty...

"C'mon..." he said as he extended his hand to help me up. I got up and he picked up the champagne flutes. I picked up the bottle and we went outside on the deck...

The fireworks had started so I was able to get lots of pictures of us with the fireworks as our backdrop. As it got closer to midnight, Darnell came up behind me again...

"Oh Darnell..." I moaned as he moved his hands up my body...

"I'm going to get inside you now..." he breathed in my ear... "And I'm going to stay inside you from this year..." he breathed as he eased himself inside me... "Into next year..." he breathed as the countdown began and he started thrusting...

"Ten..." we both panted...

"Nine..."

"Eight..."

"Seven..."

"Six..."

"Five..."

"Four..."

"Three..."

"Two..."

"One..."

"Happy New Year!"

"Huh... Huh... Huh..."

"Uuugh... Uuugh... Uuugh..."

"Darnell... Stop..."

"What's wrong?" he panted as he slowed down but didn't stop...

"Turn me around..." Darnell turned me around, I held onto the bar in back of me, and he held my legs up as he picked up where he left off... "Darnell!! Yeeesss!!"

"Uugh! Uugh! Uugh! Uugh! UUUGGGHHH!!" Darnell let my legs down, pulled me close to him, and we kissed each other profusely for the next 30 minutes or so until the fireworks began to slow down... "Happy New Year Chelle..." he said as he poured us the last of the champagne...

"Happy New Year..." Darnell..." I sighed. We finished the champagne and went back into the kitchen. Darnell started the engine and steered the yacht back towards the dock. He pulled out the flash drive, put it in his pocket, and we left the yacht...

"Oh my God... I'm so tired..." I yawned...

"So am I..." he yawned...

"I don't remember what happened after that. The next thing I remember is waking up with a hangover, in my room...

"Oh... My head..." I groaned as I tried to get up...

"Take it easy..." Darnell said as he began to rub my back...

"I can't... I gotta pee..."

"Hang on..." he said as he got up out the bed and came over to my side of the bed... "Take your time and sit up..." I sat up slowly... "How's that feel?"

"My head is spinning..."

"Wait another minute or so..."

"Okay..." I waited until the feeling subsided... "I think I can get up now..."

"Okay... take your time though..." I stood up slowly and he helped me to the bathroom...

"Where are you going?" I asked as he started getting dressed...

"I'm going to get you some coffee..."

"Hurry back..."

"I will..." he said as he closed the door and I went back to sleep...

"Chelle..." Darnell whispered...

"Huh?"

"I got you coffee..."

"Thank you..." I yawned as I sat up. I smiled when I saw that he went to Le Papillion... "Thank you Darnell..."

"You're welcome..." I got up out the bed, put on my robe, went out on the balcony, and sat at the table...

"We've been here for over a week and this is the first time we've been on the balcony..."

"This is the second time..." he corrected as he smiled at me...

"There you go again..."

"What am I doing?"

"You're making me want you..."

"So you don't want me when I'm not smiling?"

"Darnell – stop..." I laughed...

"I'm just going off what you said!" he laughed...

"Your smile... It does something to me..."

"I know..." he acknowledged as he opened our sandwiches and put them on the table...

"I was so drunk..." I laughed...

"You had a lot of champagne..."

"Yea..."

"How'd you like the yacht?"

"I loved the yacht..."

"I have something for you..." he said as he got up and went back into the room. I waited for him to come back on the balcony and when he sat down, I saw he was holding a flash drive... "This is the recording from last night..." he said as he handed it to me...

"Oohhh..."

"When we get home, we can watch it together..."

"You want me to keep it?"

"Yes..."

"Aww..." I sighed as I got up...

"Where are you going?"

"I'm going to put this in my suitcase so I don't lose it..." I answered as I went into the room. I took my suitcase out the closet, opened it, put the flash drive in the small pocket at the bottom, and put it back in the closet. When I came back out onto the balcony, Darnell noticed I was a little sad...

"What's wrong?"

"We have to leave..."

"We still have tomorrow..."

"I know..."

"Don't look at is as we have to leave – look at it as we're getting ready to talk into our future..."

"We're getting ready to walk into our future..." I sighed as we finished eating. We sat on the balcony for about another hour or so and then we decided to go back to bed...

"What time is it?" I yawned...

"It's a little after 7..." Darnell yawned...

"I can't believe we slept so long..."

"I can..."

"I'm hungry..."

"You wanna go back to Carib Sushi?"

"Yea..." I answered as I got up...

"Okay – let's take a quick shower..." he said as he got up...

"Stop it Darnell..." I said as he stood in front of me stroking his dick...

"Okay..." he laughed as we went in the bathroom and I followed...

"Darnell... Stop..." I laughed...

"Why are you telling me to stop when you don't really want me to?"

"Because we won't make it to dinner..."

"Okay – I'll stop – for now – but after dinner – you owe me dessert..." I didn't say anything – I just smiled at him mischievously...

"Stop that..."

"What am I doing?" I teased...

"Welcome back..." the waiter said as we sat down...

"Thank you..." Darnell said...

"I'll be back with your Prosecco..." he said as he walked away...

"I'm not sure I want anything to drink..." I laughed...

"You'll be fine..."

"What if I'm not?"

"I'll carry you..." I smiled at Darnell and he smiled back at me as the waiter brought our drinks to the table...

"Have you decided what you'd like to try this evening?"

"We'll have the Surf & Turf local lobster and imported tenderloin medallion..." Darnell answered...

"I'll put that right in for you..." the waiter said as he walked away and I started sipping my wine...

"This is pretty good..."

"It's nice..."

"I think I'll be okay..."

"You'd need an entire bottle to get drunk and you still wouldn't be as drunk as you were last night..."

"Did we make love?"

"You made love to your pillow as soon as your head hit it..." he laughed. The waiter brought the soup and salad and I began eating the salad... "How are you feeling?"

"You'll get dessert..." I answered as I smiled mischievously. Darnell didn't say anything – he just smiled back at me as the waiter brought the vegetable-fried rice to the table and cleared away our soup and salad bowls... "I can't wait to try the Surf & Turf..." I said as I started eating the rice...

"I'm looking forward to it..." he said as the waiter brought it to the table...

"Oh my God – this looks so good!" I exclaimed...

"Yeesss..." Darnell breathed as he tasted the lobster...

"Okay – you can't do that!" I laughed...

"I have an idea..."

"What?"

"Do you remember the scene from When Harry Met Sally?"

"Yea..."

"Let's do that..."

"Why?" I laughed...

"Cause it'll be funny..."

"Umm... Okay..." I laughed as I tasted my lobster... "Ooohhh..." I moaned. A few people looked around and Darnell covered his mouth to keep from laughing...

"Uuggghhh..." he moaned as he tasted his steak...

"Oh my God! Yeess!" I exclaimed as I tasted my steak and slumped down in my chair...

"It's sooo good!" Darnell exclaimed as he tasted his lobster again. It took everything in us to keep from laughing as we kept getting looks from other patrons...

"How's everything?" the waiter asked as he came over to our table...

"It's really good!" we both exclaimed and then we bust out laughing...

"Aaahh Haaa Haaa Haaa! Aaahh Haa Haaa Haaa!" The waiter was confused and that made us laugh even harder...

"Aaahh Haaa Haaa Haaa! Aaahh Haa Haaa Haaa!" The waiter waited for us to stop laughing and we wiped our eyes...

"I'm glad you enjoyed your food... Um... will there be anything else?"

"I'd like your fried ice cream topped with chocolate syrup!" I exclaimed...

"I'll have that too!" Darnell exclaimed as we bust out laughing again...

"Aaahh Haaa Haaa Haaa! Aaahh Haa Haaa Haaa!" The waiter shook his head and went to get our dessert...

"Excuse me..." the lady said from the table across from us...

"Yes?" I answered...

"Was it really that good?"

"Oh absolutely!"

"What'd you have?"

"Surf & Turf..."

"Oh okay – Thanks..." she said as the waiter brought our dessert and put it on the table...

"If you thought the Surf & Turf was good, try this...

"Okay..." Darnell said as he tried it first... "Oh damn!" The waiter waited for me to try it...

"Oh my God! This is delicious!"

"What's that?" somebody yelled from another table...

"Fried ice cream with chocolate syrup!" Darnell answered...

"Waiter! Over here!" somebody yelled from another table. We continued to eat our dessert as the waiter hurried from table to table and we started to feel bad...

"I didn't mean for that to happen..." Darnell sighed...

"Me either..." I agreed...

"Good evening..." the manager said as he came to our table...

"Good evening..." we both said...

"My name is Han – I wanted to come over and thank you for choosing our restaurant this week...

"You're welcome..." Darnell said...

"Tonight – Your dinner is on us..."

"Thank you!" we both exclaimed...

"You enjoyed your food so much tonight that everyone ordered the Surf & Turf... And the fried ice cream..."

"Aww... that's nice!" I exclaimed...

"You're welcome to come back anytime – enjoy your evening..." he said as he walked over to another table...

"Are you ready to go have dessert?" Darnell asked...

"Oh yesss..." I moaned and then we started laughing again on our way out the restaurant...

"Aaahh Haaa Haaa Haaa! Aaahh Haa Haaa Haaa!"

When we got back to the hotel, we went to his room...

"I can't wait to have dessert..." Darnell said as he opened the door...

"Me either..." I agreed. We stripped, got in bed, and dreamed of dessert as we both fell asleep again...

Happy New Year

"Good morning..." Darnell breathed as he kissed me awake..."

"Mmmm... Good morning..."

"You owe me dessert..."

"You want dessert?" I breathed as he began rubbing his hand up and down my body...

"Yeess..." he breathed as he put my hand on his dick...

"Beg me!" I laughed as I jumped up out the bed and hurried into the shower. Darnell was right behind me...

"You didn't think you'd get away from me that easy – did you?"

"I'm not trying to get away from you..." I breathed as I turned on the water...

"So..." he breathed as he kissed me... "Can I have dessert? Please?"

"Hmmm... Maybe..."

"Please Chelle..." he whispered as he moved my hand to his dick...

"Hmmm... Maybe..."

"Please Chelle..." he whispered as he put his hand between my legs and began rubbing my clit...

"That's... not fair..."

"All's fair in love..." he breathed as he kissed me... "And pussy..." he breathed as he continued to play with my clit...

"Oooh..." I moaned...

"Please Chelle..." he whispered as he applied more pressure...

"No..."

"What did you just say to me?" he asked as he stopped and stepped away from me...

"I said no..." I giggled...

"Fine..." he sighed as he got the loofah, lathered it up, and began to wash himself. I got the other loofah, lathered it up, and washed myself with my back to him. I was amazed that I managed to control myself when he deliberately rubbed his dick on my ass...

"Come with me..." I commanded as I pulled him by the hand into the bedroom...

"I'm coming!" he laughed...

"Not yet – get on your back!"

"Okay!" he exclaimed as he jumped on the bed and got on his back. I stood there and looked at his dick. Darnell made his dick jump a few times and I smiled as I walked over to the bed, got on the bed on my knees, and straddled him right above his dick... "Please Chelle..." he begged. I bent forward so he could ease his dick inside me. I took my time sitting up on his dick and I knew it was making him crazy... "Chelle... Please..." I sat up straight and began riding his dick slowly... "Fuck!" he moaned...

"Oh Darnell..." I moaned as I rode his dick. Darnell held me in place with his hands on my hips and allowed me to enjoy the ride... "Huh... Huh... Huh..."

"Chelle... Ugghhh..."

"Harder... I'm cumming..." Darnell began to thrust himself up inside me so hard we rose up off the bed with each thrust... "Haa! Haa! Haa! Haa! Haaaaa!"

"Uggh! Uggh! Uggh! Uggh! UUUGGGHHH!"

"Oh Darnell..." I sighed as I bent down to lay on him. Darnell held me and we continued to lay there for a few moments...

"We need to go back in the shower..."

"I know..." I didn't want to get up and he knew it. In that moment I realized I was falling in love with him and I think he knew it too...

"Let's go get in the shower so we can get brunch..."

"Okay..." I sighed as I got up. I looked down at Darnell and smiled before I got up off him and then we went back into the bathroom and got in the shower...

It was after 12 when we left the hotel so we decided to go back to Umbrellas...

"Welcome back – what would you like to try today?" the waitress asked as she placed our cappuccinos on the table...

"I'll have the lobster grilled with garlic butter, sweet potato fries, and Caesar salad..." I answered...

"And for you Sir?"

"I'll have the grilled shrimp with shoestring fries, and grilled garlic bread..." Darnell answered...

"I'll be right back..." she said as she went to place our order...

"What would you like to do today?" Darnell asked...

"Since today's our last day, I'd like to have some Rum Punch..." I sighed...

"Are you sure?"

"Yea..."

"Are you okay?"

"I'm okay – I just don't wanna go back to work..." I sighed...

"Neither do I..." he added as the waitress brought our food to the table...

"Woa - I didn't think there'd be this much food!" I exclaimed...

"Enjoy!" the waitress said as she walked away and went to another table. We sat there for a while and took our time enjoying our food. When we were done, the waitress came back over to the table...

"All set?"

"We'd like some Rum Punch..." I answered...

"Coming right up..." she said as she continued to clear the table. After she brought our drinks to the table, we sat there for nearly an hour enjoying the view as we sipped. It was almost 3 p.m. when we finally got up to leave...

"Where should we go now?" Darnell asked...

"Let's go back to the beach..." I sighed as I took his hand. We took our time walking to the beach and when we got there, Darnell walked us over to the spot behind the rocks where we made love in the water, we sat down, and I laid in his arms until the sun began to set...

"You wanna go to Esther's for one last drink?"

"Yea..." I sighed as we got up...

"Welcome back! Shall I get you your usual?" the bartender asked...

"Yes – I'd like another Screaming Orgasm!" I exclaimed as everyone laughed...

"And for you sir?"

"I'd like my last Adios Motherfucker!" Darnell exclaimed...

"Is this your last night here?"

"Yes..."

"Adios Motherfucker!" everyone exclaimed and then we all bust out laughing...

"We stumbled back to his room, stripped out of our clothes, climbed into bed, and fell asleep...

"Good morning..." Darnell breathed as he kissed me awake...

"Good morning..." I yawned. We both got up out of bed and went to take a shower without our usual play...

"I can't believe it's time to check out..." he sighed...

"We can always come back..." I said as I smiled. Darnell smiled back at me and it brightened my mood as we continued to pack... "Time to go to my room..." I sighed as we left his room and went to my room. Darnell sat on the chaise lounge as I packed my suitcase. I was glad I didn't bring that much to begin with so everything we bought fit inside...

"You ready?"

"I'm ready." We went downstairs, dropped our keys in the drop box, and left the resort...

"Delta 583 now boarding at Airbus A319." We got up, Darnell took my hand, and we headed towards the gate. Our seats were in the back of the plane this time but we didn't mind because our plan was to sleep anyway. We woke up just as the flight attendant announced we were landing in Atlanta...

"Damn I'm hungry!" I exclaimed...

"I know just the place..." Darnell laughed as we headed towards the Atlanta Chophouse & Brewery...

"I think I'm going to like this..."

"You will – You'll be full too so when we get in later tonight you won't need to stop and eat again...

"Welcome to the Chophouse – May I start you off with something to drink?"

"I'll have a ginger ale..." I answered...

"I'll have a Pepsi..." Darnell answered...

"I'll be right back..." the waiter said as he went to get our drinks...

"I can't believe we're home..."

"I know – right?"

"It feels weird..."

"It does..."

"Here you are..." the waiter said as he placed our drinks on the table... "Have you had a chance to look over the menu?"

"Yes – I'll have the Chophouse Burger with cheddar – well done – and white rice pilaf..." I answered...

"And you Sir?"

"I'll have the Shaved Prime Rib minus the horseradish mayo – and white cheddar mashed potatoes..." Darnell answered...

"Okay..." the waiter said as he went to place our order...

"I love the way you ride dick..." Darnell whispered...

"Me too..."

"You were so wet..." he whispered as he took my hand and started rubbing it...

"I know..."

"I love watching you enjoy yourself..."

"I love enjoying myself..."

"Can I ask you a personal question?"

"Sure..."

"How long as it been?"

"It's been a while..." I answered as the waiter put our food on the table...

"Can I get you a refill on your drinks?" he asked...

"Yes please..." we both answered. The waiter went to get our refills and we started eating...

"Delta 1143 now boarding at Boeng 717." We got up, Darnell took my hand, we boarded the plane, and we realized we both had window seats on opposite sides of the plane...

"Excuse me – would you mind if we switched seats so I can sit with my lady?" Darnell asked the gentleman sitting next to me...

"If she's your lady why didn't you buy seats next to each other?"

"We had to take what was left... Darnell sighed...

"What if I don't wanna move?" the gentleman snapped...

"Fuck it – I'll move – Miss – If you give me your window seat you can sit with your man..." the gentleman sitting next to Darnell said...

"I'll take the window seat – you can have my seat..." the gentleman said sitting next to me...

"Oh no you won't – My man asked you to move and you didn't want to – he gets my window seat!" I exclaimed as I stood up and pointed to the gentleman sitting next to Darnell...

"Is there a problem?" the stewardess asked as she came over...

"No problem at all – I'm giving my window seat to that gentleman so I can sit with my man..." I answered...

"We have two seats in the back of the plane if you'd like..."

"I'll take those – All this conversation between them is getting on my nerves!" the gentleman sitting next to me exclaimed as he unbuckled his belt, jumped up, and stormed towards the back of the plane as everyone clapped...

"Thank you..." Darnell said as he got up... "You can have my window seat..." he said to the gentleman sitting next to him...

"No problem..." the gentleman said as he got up and let Darnell out into the aisle. Darnell sat down beside me, we buckled our seat belts, and I snuggled up underneath him as they prepared for takeoff...

Happy New Year

"I can't wait to get off the plane – I'm so tired!" I exclaimed as I stood up..."

"I'm so tired – I wish I could stay at your house..." Darnell sighed...

"I wish you could stay with me too – but I don't think your wife would appreciate that..." I said as I took my bag out from under the seat. Darnell took his bag out from under his seat, we both stepped out into the isle, and then we exited the plane...

"That's him..." the flight attendant said as she pointed towards us. We both stopped as two police officers approached us...

"Darnell Tompkins?"

"Yes?"

"We need you to come with us..." Officer Nunn said as he went to touch Darnell's arm...

"Excuse me – am I under arrest?"

"No... But we need you to come with us please..."

"Darnell – is everything okay?"

"Who are you Maam?"

"I'm his girlfriend..." Officer Sullivan shook his head and I was confused...

"Wait here..." Officer Nunn commanded...

"I need you to tell me what's going on or I'm not going with you..." Darnell said...

"I'm Officer Nunn, this is Officer Sullivan..."

"Nice to meet you both but you still haven't told me why you need me to go with you..."

"We need to speak to you about your wife..." Officer Nunn answered...

"Dana?! Of my God – What happened?!"

"Please come with us..." Officer Nunn asked. Darnell followed them and my heart sank...

"What's wrong with my wife?!"

"I'm sorry to tell you this..." Officer Nunn started to say..."

"Noooo!!" Darnell cried as he broke down..."

"I'm sorry..."

"When?!"

"Your neighbor Helen found her on Christmas eve..." Officer Sullivan answered....

"Oh my God! Where is she?!"

"She's in the City Morgue in New Rochelle..." Officer Nunn answered..."

"She's been in the morgue all this time... and I was with someone else..."

"Is that your girlfriend out there?" Officer Sullivan asked...

"Yea..."

"Does she know you're married?!" Officer Nunn asked...

"She knows..."

"We know you asked for wife for a divorce..."

"How do you know that?!"

"We found the letter you wrote your wife along with the divorce papers..." Officer Sullivan answered...

"We also know your wife was having an affair..." Officer Nunn added...

"I guess you saw the picture..."

"We saw the picture, we read your letter, and we also read the text message your wife received..." Officer Sullivan added...

"How did my wife die?"

"We're waiting for the coroner to confirm, but we believe it was an accident..." Officer Nunn answered...

"An accident?'

"Yes – your wife's medication was on the counter along with a bottle of champagne and a champagne flute – there was blood in the countertop and on the floor..."

"So she fell?"

"It looked like she slipped and hit her head on the counter before she hit the floor..."

"What do you mean looked like?"

"We took photos..." Officer Sullivan answered as he showed the pictures to Darnell...

"Oh my God... Dana... I'm sorry..." he whispered as he cried...

"Your neighbor saw her on the floor and called us – she had a key..."

"I should've been here..."

"Mr. Tompkins – you had no way of knowing this was going to happen..." Officer Nunn said...

"Chelle was right – I'm a coward – I should've had a conversation with her – I should've been here!"

"Mr. Tompkins – even if you were here – you probably would've ended up fighting – you would've left – this could've happened anyway – please don't blame yourself..." Officer Sullivan said...

"I have to make arrangements..."

"Here – take your wife's things..." Officer Sullivan said as he gave Darnell the divorce papers, the letter, and her phone in a plastic bag... "Go home – clean up your house – and try to get some sleep – you can't do anything tonight – wait until tomorrow morning..." he advised...

Happy New Year

"Thank you..." Darnell said as he took the bag and got up to leave...

"How do you think his girlfriend will take the news?" Officer Sullivan asked...

"She'll be there for him, she'll love him, and then she'll marry him..."

"Wow!"

"Happens all the time..." Officer Nunn said as they got up to leave...

"Chelle..."

"Darnell?! What's wrong?!"

"Sit with me... Please..." I sat with him and took his hands in mine...

"My wife..."

"What happened?"

"She's dead..." he whispered as he started crying...

"Oh Darnell... I'm sorry..."

"She was drinking champagne... she slipped... she hit her head on the counter..." I pulled him into a hug and held him as he cried... "She died on Christmas Eve – she's been in the morgue the whole time I was with you!"

"I'm sorry Darnell..." I whispered as I started crying...

"No... I'm sorry... It's not your fault... I didn't mean to take it out on you..."

"That's okay... I understand... I'll let you go..."

"No Chelle – Please don't leave me – I need you..."

"I was going to tell you I didn't want us to see each other while you were still married – and now that I know she's dead..."

"Please Chelle – Don't leave me – I just need time to make the arrangements...

"Darnell – Listen..."

"Okay..."

"I only wanted us to take a break until after you finalized your divorce. Now that she's dead – I don't want us to see each other until after the funeral..."

"So you'll wait for me?"

"Yes Darnell – I'll wait for you..."

"Can I call you?"

"I don't think we should call each other right now – but you can text me if you need to..."

"I have to go home..."

"I know..."

"I don't wanna do this..."

"I wish I could be there with you – but I can't..." I said as I stood up to leave and he stood up to...

"You're gonna wait for me – right?"

"Yes Darnell..." Darnell pulled me into a hug and kissed me hard... Darnell... I need to go..."

"I'll see you Monday..."

"Monday?"

"Yes... I'll see you Monday..." I started crying as I walked away from him. As bad as I wanted to turn and run back to him – I knew better...

"Dana..." Darnell cried as he went inside... "I'm so sorry..." he cried as he looked at the blood on the counter and the floor. He went over to the counter, picked up her prescription bottles, went to the bathroom, put them in the medicine cabinet, and went back into the kitchen. He got the 409 out the cabinet, cleaned her blood off the counter, put it back under the sink, and threw the sponge away. He took the Swiffer out the closet and began to cry as he cleaned her blood up off the floor... "Damn Dana – It wasn't supposed to end like this – I loved you..." He continued using the Swiffer, changing the pads until he was satisfied there wasn't any blood left, and then he put the Swiffer away. He stopped to look at the bottle of champagne on the counter and picked it up... "Let's finish what you started..." he said as he poured some champagne into the champagne flute and gulped it down... "Wooo... Not done yet!" he exclaimed as he poured the rest of the champagne into the champagne flute and picked it up... "Well Dana... This is it... The end of a decade..." he slurred as he gulped down the champagne and threw the champagne flute in the garbage. He picked up the empty bottle and threw it in the garbage so hard he broke the bottle and the glass... "Hmmph!" he exclaimed as he took the letter, divorce papers, and phone out the plastic bag... "Let's see what this text was all about..." he slurred as he sat down at the island and began reading the text...

Happy New Year

"Dana,

It's over between us. Your husband sent my wife a picture of us in front of the hotel and she went ballistic. If I had known this when I saw him at the hotel yesterday I would've knocked the shit out of him because that's a bitch-ass move – he should've been man enough to confront me when he saw me but instead – he told me to tell my wife he said hello.

I know this isn't your fault and I'm not blaming you at all – I blame myself because it's my fault. I never should've started seeing you in the first place – especially because we work together – but I was weak when it came to you and instead of using logic and common sense, I let my other head lead me into trouble.

I'm going to spend every waking moment trying to make this up to my wife. She deserves better and I'm praying she can forgive me. I suggest you try and work things out with your husband if you can.

Kevin"

"Well Dana – you got dumped by both of us – Merry Fuckin' Christmas – It was Merry – And I was definitely fuckin' – And Happy Fuckin' New Year – And trust me when I tell you – I brought the New Year in very happy – And I was Fuckin'!" he exclaimed... "What's that? You didn't make it to Christmas? You didn't live to see the New Year? Sucks to be you I guess – Now I gotta bury your ass – I should be knee-deep in pussy right now but no – you had to be the bane of my existence – You couldn't let me bring the New Year in without doing something to fuck it up – Fuck you and fuck him too – I loved you with all my heart – And you broke it Dana!" he exclaimed as he broke down...

"Hey Chelle..."

"Hey..." I cried...

"You found out – didn't you?"

"Found out what?"

"You found out who Darnell is..."

"You knew?"

"Yea..."

"I didn't know Veronica – I swear..."

"I know you didn't – but now that you know who he is – you know you gotta leave him alone – right?"

"I can't..."

"He's married to Dana!"

"Not anymore..."

"What's that supposed to mean?"

"Can you come over?"

"You want me to come to your house?! Now?! Do you know what time it is?!"

"Never mind..."

"I'll come over..."

"Never mind..."

"You still wanna talk?"

"Yea..."

"Okay..."

"I'm gonna tell you a lot – but you can't tell anybody!"

"You really think I would tell people you were in Bermuda with Darnell?!"

"That's not what I'm talking about..."

"Oh – 'cause I was about to go off on your ass!"

"You still might..." I sniffed...

"Girl – what happened?!"

"How much time do you have?"

"Fuck it – I got all night – what happened?"

'Okay – I got in my Uber to go the airport..."

"On Saturday?"

"Yea..."

"Okay..."

"So we're at the light and Darnell starts tapping on the window..."

"He was in White Plains?!"

"Yea – he said his Uber cancelled and he needed to get to the airport..."

"That's crazy!"

"The Uber driver said he couldn't take him and Darnell told him he'd pay him $100..."

"Oh shit!"

"So I told the driver I was going to the airport too, the driver let him get in, he introduced himself, and then he kissed my hand..."

"That was nice..."

"It sure was – when I felt his breath on my hand – oh my God!"

"You was ready to fuck him – right?"

"Yes!"

"Damn!"

"So we get to the airport and he reimburses me for the Uber and gives me extra money for my kindness..."

"Damn – he was feelin' you!"

"So we talked a little and that's when I found out he was on my flight..."

"To Bermuda?"

"Yea..."

"That doesn't make any sense – unless he was planning to go down there to hoe around..."

"I hope not..."

"Isn't that what you were going down there to do?!"

"No!"

"I thought you were looking for Dexter?"

"I was!"

"Well then – you were going to hoe around!"

"I only wanted Dexter!" I laughed...

"Okay – I need to know how you wound up with Darnell..."

"Okay – so Darnell told me he went to Kay Jewelers to buy his wife a tennis bracelet..."

"Okay..."

"So he thought his wife was cheating on him so he had his lawyer follow her and he sent Darnell a picture..."

"Oh shit!! She was cheating on him?!"

"Yea... and it broke his heart..."

"Damn..."

"So he bought the bracelet anyway and then he went home, wrote her a letter, told her he wanted a divorce, printed divorce papers off the computer, filled them out, signed them, and left them there with his ring and a pen!"

"Ooohhh sshhiiittt!!"

"I was mad at him until I found out why he did it the way he did it but then I got mad at her and told him I wanted to slap her!"

"Damn! So now you wanna slap Dana!"

"I didn't know who she was!"

"He didn't tell you?!"

'No! But I didn't ask..."

"You didn't want to know?!"

"No..."

"You better than me..."

"Veronica – we just met!"

"Okay – you right – but you knew he was married – and you still wanted to fuck him – right?"

"Yea..."

"Okay – I just wanted to make sure I understood that part..."

"So I went to get us coffee at Starbucks..."

"Okay..."

"And the cashier tells me Darnell is my husband..."

"She thought he was your husband?"

"No – she told me he was my husband – she said she saw him propose to me!"

"That's crazy – I bet she told you she was psychic – right?"

"She told me she was sensitive and she could see things..."

"I'm sensitive – I can see things too – And I see she's full of shit!"

"I don't know about that..."

"You believe her?"

"Yea..."

"Damn – you got dickmatized..."

"It's more than that Veronica..."

"I just can't believe you fell for that..."

"Veronica! Listen!"

"Okay – I'm listening..."

"So I give him the coffee and he tells me if I was his lady he wouldn't let me out of his sight..."

"You believed him – right?"

"Yea..."

"I knew it – go ahead..."

"So we get to the desk to board and they call me up to the counter..."

"What happened?!"

"Darnell upgraded our tickets to first class..."

"Damn – he was reeling you in..."

"It's not like that!"

"If you say so..."

"He kissed me..."

"Like I said... reeling you in..."

"We sat together on the plane..."

"Mmm Hmm – go ahead..."

"We stayed at the same hotel..."

"Mmm Hmm..."

"Our rooms were on the same floor..."

"Mmm Hmm..."

"We did it in my room first..."

"Uh Huh..."

"Then we did it in his room..."

"And then you did it on the beach..."

"Yea..."

"Okay – you went to Bermuda to find Dexter – you found Dexter – I get it – but now you're back here – back to reality – he's married to Dana – Hellooo!!"

"Veronica?"

"Yes?"

"Remember I told you he bought that tennis bracelet?"

"Yea?"

"He gave it to me..."

"He gave you a bracelet he bought for his wife?!"

"That's what I thought too – but he said he bought the bracelet for the woman that was going to be his Now & Forever..."

"Okay – don't take this the wrong way..."

"Okay..."

"What if he bought a fake bracelet to bring to Bermuda to give to the first woman who gave him pussy?"

"I don't believe that..."

"Okay – how 'bout this – you said he went to Kay Jewelers – right?"

"Yea..."

"Okay - take the bracelet to Kay Jewelers – tell them you want a certificate of authenticity – if they give you one then you know he was telling you the truth..."

"Okay – I'll do that..."

"Okay – so he gave you the bracelet – so you're his Now & Forever?"

"He said I gave myself to him so I was his... now... and forever..." I sniffed...

"Damn! Either he got good game or he's really falling for you..."

"I hope he's really falling for me..."

"I hope so too – but he's still married!"

"Not anymore..."

"Why do you keep saying that?!"

"Don't tell anybody..."

"I swear to God – if you don't tell me what happened right now – I'm hanging up!"

"When we got to the airport the police were waiting for Darnell..."

"Oh shit – why?"

"They said they needed to talk to him about his wife... and I heard him say Dana..."

"So that's when you found out he was married to Dana..."

"Yea..."

"Why did the police wanna talk to Darnell?"

"Dana's dead..."

"WHAT?!"

"Her neighbor found her in the house on Christmas Eve..."

"Did Darnell kill her?!"

"No – she slipped and hit her head on the counter..."

"So the whole time y'all were fuckin' in Bermuda – she was in the morgue!"

"Yea..." I sighed as I started crying...

"Damn – that's fucked up..."

"I never wanted her to die..."

"I know you didn't..."

"He just wanted a divorce..."

"Did he show you the picture?"

"No – why?"

"Well – I'm just gonna say it – she was fuckin' Kevin!"

"At 112?!"

"Yup!"

"Damn – I thought Kevin was so nice!"

"He is nice – he was just fuckin' Dana!"

"Are you sure?"

"Let me put it to you like this – a lot of people were talkin' about how she was always in his office after 5 with the door closed..."

"I think it's true..."

"You do?"

"Yea..."

"What makes you say that?"

"Darnell told me he knew the guy in the picture – and he knows the guy's wife..."

"Oh shit!"

"He wants me to wait for him..."

"Wait for him?! For what?!"

"He wants me to wait for him while he makes the arrangements so he can bury her..."

"So you're gonna wait for him?!"

"Yea..." I sighed...

"I'm done – I'm going to bed – I'll see you tomorrow..."

"Please don't be mad at me..."

"Good night Chelle..." she said as she hung up...

"Good morning..." I greeted as I walked in...

"Hey Chelle!" Veronica greeted... "I put your box on your desk for you..."

"Thank you Veronica." I went over to my new desk, took out a bottle of 409, and began spraying the desk...

"You don't need to do that – that desk was cleaned a while ago..." he said. Veronica looked at him and looked back at me...

"Veronica – do you have any paper towels?" I asked...

"Here..." she answered as she handed me a roll...

"Thanks..." I said as I took the roll from her, took a few sheets, and wiped the desk down.

I opened the drawers, took the bottle of 409, and started spraying again...

"You really don't need to do that – those drawers haven't been opened in weeks..."

"Is this bothering you?" I asked...

"Why would it be bothering me?"

"I figured it was bothering you because you keep commenting on it..."

"You don't need to get smart – I was just letting you know the desk was clean..."

"Who said I was getting smart?" I asked as Stephen came in...

"Good morning – I'm Stephen Richards – Welcome to 85 – you must be Chelle..." he said as he extended his hand to shake mine...

"Good morning – Thank you – I'm Chelle..." I acknowledged as I shook his hand...

"I'll let you get settled – come see me when you're ready..." he said as he went into his office...

"I like him already..." I sighed as I continued to clean the desk drawers. When I was done, I gave Veronica the paper towels... "Thank you Veronica..."

"You're welcome..." she said as I got up and went into Stephen's office...

"You unpacked already?"

"No – I can do that later..."

"Are you sure?"

"I'm sure..."

"Okay then – let me get you up to speed..."

167

"Okay..." I said as I picked up his pad and took a pen out his cup holder... "Do you mind?"

"Not at all..." he answered as he smiled. I knew he was impressed... "I was told you worked for Dana Tompkins at 112..."

"I did..."

"Did you supervise any clerical staff?"

"No..."

"Do you have any supervisor experience?"

"No..."

"As my administrative assistant, you'll be supervising Veronica and Ronald..."

"I know Veronica..." I said as I smiled...

"How do you know her?"

"She's my best friend..."

"Is that going to be a problem for you?"

"If she's anything like me – it shouldn't be a problem..."

"What does that mean?"

"If she comes to work on time, does her work, and stays on top of her work, it won't be a problem..."

"What if she has a problem with you being her supervisor?"

"Sucks to be her then..." I laughed...

"Wow – I didn't expect that..."

"I'm sorry – I know from experience that you may not always like who you work with – but I also understand we don't get paid to like each other..."

"Hmmm... okay... so... about Ronald..."

"He's something else..." I laughed...

"So you met him?"

"No..."

"What happened?"

"I was cleaning my new desk and he told me I didn't need to do that because the desk was already clean..."

"That was your introduction?"

"Yes – and when I asked him if it was bothering him he asks why would it bother me so I told him I figured it was bothering him because he mentioned it..."

"How'd he respond?"

"He told me I didn't need to get smart because he was just trying to tell me the desk was clean..."

"I'm so sick of him – I'm sorry you had to experience that..."

"I'm not..."

"You're not?"

"Nope – I know exactly who he is and I'll treat him accordingly..."

"I like you..."

"I like you too..."

"So now let's talk about what you'll be doing for me..."

"Okay..."

"Veronica has been doing the stats and monthly reports – you'll be taking over that responsibility..."

"Okay..." I acknowledged as I began writing...

"Veronica also orders supplies, covers reception when they need assistance, processes applications, and helps Ronald with the mail scanning, and indexing..."

"I have a question..."

"Go ahead..."

"What does Ron do?"

"Ron does the mail, scanning, indexing, and rotates covering reception when they need assistance..."

"I have another question..."

"Go ahead..."

"Why does Veronica help Ron with his work in addition to doing her own work? Is it that much or is he lazy?"

"I'll let you see for yourself..."

"I have another question..."

'Go ahead..."

"Does Veronica prepare packets for stat meetings or is that my responsibility?"

"That'll be your responsibility but Veronica will help you when you need it..."

"Okay – I have another question..."

"Go ahead..."

"Can I work 9 to 5?"

"I was hoping you'd be willing to work 9 to 5..."

"You were?"

"Yes – Veronica works 8 to 4 and Ronald works 8:30 to 4:30..."

"Do we sign in or clock in?"

"We clock in..."

"Okay – I have another question..."

"Go ahead..."

"Is it okay if I meet with them and make a few changes?"

"You wanna make changes? Already?"

"Yes..."

"What would you like to change?"

"I'd like to have Ron cover reception on a regular basis..."

"So you want to take Veronica out of the rotation?"

"Yes..."

"Why?"

"I think it would serve you better to have Veronica cover in my absence and be my back up when needed – Ron can handle covering reception because it's not difficult – it's actually easier than covering the commissioner's office at lunch...

"Oh boy – Ron's not going to like that..."

"I don't mean any disrespect – but we don't always get paid to do what we like..."

"I think you're going to end up bumping heads with him – but you're his new supervisor – if that's what you want to do – it's fine..."

"Thanks – I have another question..."

"Okay – go ahead..."

"Is there a particular time you'd prefer I don't take vacation?"

"I don't understand the question..."

"At 112, we had to rotate who got to take Thanksgiving, Christmas, and the week after New Year...."

"As long as we have coverage, I'm flexible – but you and I can't be out at the same time – I need coverage – especially since you're their new supervisor..."

"I just realized something..."

"What's that?"

"You haven't been able to take any time off..."

"No I haven't..."

"Are you taking any time off soon?"

"I'm taking next week..."

"So you're taking form January 9th through January 16th and you'll be back on Tuesday – January 17th..."

"Yes..."

"Okay – I'll put that on the calendar..."

"I do my own calendar..."

"Not anymore you don't..." I said as I kept writing...

"How does that work?"

"You go in outlook, you give me access to your calendar, and I'll add meetings, annual leave, etc. to your calendar for you..."

"Okay..." he acknowledged as he nodded his head...

"Oh – one more thing..."

"Go ahead..."

"At 112, some people would clock in and then go out for coffee – I'm going to let them know they can't do that..." Stephen didn't say anything. He just shook his head and started laughing...

"What's so funny?"

"Ronald isn't going to like you..."

"Oh – one more question..."

"Go ahead..."

"Veronica and I go to lunch together a lot – can we still do that?"

"As long as I have coverage..."

"So I have to check with Ron..." I sighed...

"Exactly..."

"What are the lunch hours?"

"Lunch is between 12 and 2 – why?"

"Sometimes I make appointments at lunch and they go over an hour..."

"Does it happen every day?"

"No..."

"As long as it doesn't happen every day, it's fine..."

"I use my time when it happens too..."

"Good – this way when Ronald comes tattling I can ignore it..." I didn't respond. I just continued writing until I was finished...

"Is there a room I can meet with them in?"

"You can use my office if you'd like..."

"I can? That's nice – thanks..."

"You're welcome – but I have an ulterior motive..."

"What's the ulterior motive?"

"I'm going to sit at your desk so I can hear Ronald's reaction to your changes..." he laughed as he got up...

"Thank you for coming..." I said as I handed them both a pad and a pen...

"What's this for?" Ron asked...

"I gave you a pad and a pen so you can write down the changes I'm going to make and you can also write down any questions you have..." I answered...

"Changes? You just got here!"

""Let me introduce myself. I'm Chelle Robinson, your new supervisor..."

"I'm Veronica Humphrey, your office assistant..."

"I'm Ronald Nelson. I'm the office clerk..."

"Nice to meet you Ron – is it okay if I call you Ron?"

"Yes – that's fine..."

"I already know Veronica..."

"Okay — now that you've introduced yourself – what changes are you going to make?" Ron asked...

"The first thing I want to address is clocking in when you come to work..."

"I clock in every day..." Ron interrupted...

"Please let me finish..."

'Okay...'

"At 112, people would clock in and then go back out for coffee..."

"What's wrong with that?"

"I stop to get my coffee or breakfast before I clock in – I don't clock in and then go back out to get coffee..."

"So I have to stop and get my coffee before I come in – that's going to make me late for work..."

"If it makes you late for work, then you need to leave earlier or wait until it's break time to get your coffee..."

"Are you serious?!"

"Yes..." I saw Veronica smirk but I acted as if I didn't see it... "Okay – Now I'd like to address your hours..."

"I work 8:30 to 4:30..." Ron interjected...

"Veronica – what hours do you work?"

"I work 8 to 4..."

"Okay – I'll be working 9 to 5..." I waited for Ron to finish writing and then I continued... "Veronica – I'll start with you..."

"Oh we about to fight!" she laughed...

"Effective immediately – I'll be taking over the stats and the monthly reports..."

"Yes!"

"You'll continue to order the supplies and process applications..."

"Okay..."

"You're also going to continue to assist when it's time to prepare the packets for stat meetings..."

"I do that anyway..."

"That's not what I said..."

"My bad – what did you say?"

"I said you'll assist in preparing the packets..."

"Oh so I don't have to do it all myself?"

"No – you'll be assisting me in preparing the packets..."

"Okay!"

"You'll also be my back-up in my absence..."

"Your back-up?"

"Yes - When I'm out, you'll be covering for Stephen..."

"Oh okay – so instead of doing that full-time, I'll only do that when you're not here..."

"Exactly..."

"What about when she has to cover reception?" Ron asked. I saw the look Veronica gave him and I didn't blame her...

"I'm glad you asked me that..."

"Why?"

"Effective immediately – Veronica is out of the rotation for covering reception..."

"WHAT?!" they both exclaimed...

"Ron – You'll stay in the rotation to cover reception..."

"That's not fair – why am I the only one that has to cover reception?!"

"As I said – I'm making changes..."

"This some bullshit..." he mumbled...

"Excuse me?!" I snapped...

"Nothing..."

"Also – Effective immediately – You'll be doing the mail, scanning, and indexing by yourself..."

"Yes! Oh – sorry..." Veronica said...

"Why can't Veronica help me with the mail, scanning, and indexing?"

"Do you help Veronica do any of her work?"

"No – But..."

"Exactly..." I interrupted. Veronica was beaming from ear to ear and Ron was seething... "That's all for now – Veronica – I need to speak to you privately..." Ron got up and stormed out the office...

"Girl – he is pissed!"

"I know – I need you to do something for me..."

"Yes?"

"I need you to send me the stats and the monthly reports..."

"Okay..."

"I also need you to update the org chart..."

"Okay..."

"And I need you to draft a memo from me to reception to let them know effective immediately you are out of the rotation for covering reception and make sure you put in the memo that Ronald Nelson will be in the rotation permanently..."

"What if Ron's out and they want me to cover?"

"Hopefully I can keep you out of it but if you're assisting me with the stats or the monthly reports, or packets – you're not covering..."

"What if Steph says I have to cover?"

"I discussed all the changes with him before we met and he approved the changes..."

"Okay! I'm glad you're here!"

"I'm glad I'm here too..."

"Thank God I don't have to help Ron anymore..."

"You have enough to do as it is..."

"Exactly!"

"Okay – we'll talk more later – Steph said we can go to lunch if you want so I need you to get started..."

"I'll do the memo first – I know Ron is pissed!"

"Make sure you cc Ron and Stephen too..."

"I sure will!" she exclaimed as she got up...

"Before you leave I need to address one more thing – vacations..."

"Ron always takes Christmas Eve..."

"I need you to prepare a schedule so we can rotate holidays..."

"How do I do that? Do I put it on a calendar?"

"No – send me the schedule of the holidays and who took what days so far – I'll take it from there..."

"Okay..."

"Oh – One more thing – Who does payroll?"

'I do..." Veronica answered....

"Not anymore – I'll be doing the payroll from now on..."

"Thank you!" she exclaimed...

"I need you to go in leave management, remove yourself, and add me..."

"Okay!" Stephen waited for her to leave and then he came inside...

"That went well..." I said...

"I heard..." he laughed...

"I told Veronica I'll be taking over the payroll..."

"That's fine..."

"I also told her to draft a memo from me to reception to let them know effective immediately she's out of the rotation and Ron is in the rotation permanently..."

"That's fine too..."

"She's worried that they'll try to make her cover if Ron is out but I told her if she's backing me up or assisting me with stats, she's not going..."

"That's fine..."

"Okay – I'm going to unpack and set up my desk so I can get to work – I'll see you later Stephen..."

"Steph..."

"Okay Steph..." I spent the rest of the morning laughing to myself as I unpacked and set up my desk. Ron was busy slamming mail, his desk drawers, the copy machine drawers, and anything else he felt like slamming... "How's it going?"

"It's going!" he snapped...

"Are you almost done with the mail?"

"Does it look like I'm almost done?!" he exclaimed...

"It looks like you need to move a little faster so you can get the mail done before you go to lunch..." I answered as I went back to putting my desk together. I didn't notice Steph was standing there...

The rest of the morning was quiet other than Ron continuing to slam things around. I started thinking about what Veronica told me to do and at the last minute, I decided not to go to lunch with her...

"I'm ready to go to lunch..." she said...

"I'm not going to be able to go to lunch with you..."

"Is everything okay?"

"Everything's okay..." I answered without looking up. Veronica shrugged her shoulders and left for lunch. As soon as she left, I got up and left behind her...

Happy New Year

"Welcome to Kay Jewelers – Oh hey!" Cindy beamed when she saw me...

"Hey..."

"How's the bracelet?"

"Still beautiful..." I sighed...

"That's great – what can I do for you today?"

"I need a certificate of authenticity..."

"You'll get that in the mail – we don't have those here..."

"Oh shoot..." I sighed...

"You're not doubting us – are you?"

"No – it's just – never mind..."

"What's wrong?"

"I got this bracelet for Christmas..." I answered as I took the bracelet out the box...

"Oh my God! I remember when he bought that!"

"You do?!"

"Yes! You must be his Now & Forever!"

"How'd you know that?!"

"Oh shoot – I shouldn't've said anything!"

"Why?!"

"Okay – I'm going to tell you – but please don't tell him I told you..."

"Okay..."

"He bought that bracelet on Friday..."

"Friday? December 23rd?"

"Yes – I told him it was from our Now & Forever Collection and he said he wanted to buy it..."

"Aww..."

"I told him his wife was a lucky woman because I thought he was going to give it to his wife but he said the only thing his wife was getting for Christmas from him was a divorce..." I couldn't hold back the tears...

"Oh my God – what's wrong?!" she asked as she came from behind the counter and hugged me...

"Nothing..." I sniffed. Cindy picked up a box of tissues and gave it to me so I could blow my nose...

"You're not crying for nothing..."

"I can't help it – I'm so happy..."

"I just told you that the man that gave you that bracelet is married – and you're happy?"

"I'm crying because you just confirmed he was telling the truth..."

"Ooohhh..."

"He gave me this bracelet on Christmas Day... He told me I was his Now & Forever..." I sighed as I continued crying..."

"Aww..." she sighed as she began tearing up... "I can check to see if the certificate's been mailed out if you want..."

"No – I'll wait for him to give it to me..."

"Okay – Do you need help with anything else?"

"Actually... Yes – I do need your help with something..."

"What can I do for you?"

"I want to buy that ring over there..." I answered as I pointed to the men's diamond ½ ct round cut 10k two-tone gold ring...

"Oh wow – that the perfect complement to your bracelet!" she exclaimed...

"Yes it is..." I sighed...

"Are you going to give it to him today?" she asked...

"Nope – I'm going to wait until he proposes to me..."

"Oh wow! You think he's going to propose?"

"Well – he did say I was his Now & Forever..."

"Yes he did! I'll get that boxed for you right away!"

"Thank you..." I sighed. I noticed Cindy was crying as she was preparing my purchase and I was a bit curious but I didn't ask her about it...

"Here you are..."

"Thank you..." I sighed as I stuffed the bag in my purse...

"You're welcome..." she said as I turned to leave and walked out...

"She has no idea what's coming..." Cindy whispered...

I hurried down to the food court, ordered a chicken steak and kiwi lemonade to go from Charlies, and hurried back to work...

As soon as I got back to work, I went over to Veronica's desk...

"Yes?" she asked...

"I need to talk to you – where do we eat at?"

"I'll show you were the break room is..." she answered as she got up. I followed her to the break room and as soon as we got in there, I sat down and started crying again...

"What happened?!" she exclaimed as she sat down at the table with me...

"I went to Kay Jewelers..."

"Oh no..."

"I asked Cindy for a certificate of authenticity for the bracelet..."

"Damn... I'm sorry Chelle..."

"He was telling the truth..."

"WHAT?!"

"Cindy told him his wife was a lucky woman because she thought he was buying the bracelet for her – but he told her the only thing his wife was getting from him for Christmas was a divorce!"

"Oh shit! Okay!"

"He told Cindy he was buying the bracelet for the woman that was going to be his Now & Forever!" I exclaimed as I continued crying...

"Damn – I'm so happy for you I don't know what to do!' she exclaimed as she hugged me and started crying...

"Is everything okay?" Steph asked as he came into the break room...

"Yea – I'm sorry – I just got back from lunch – I didn't get a chance to eat..." I answered...

"Well you don't need to cry about it - hurry up and eat!" he exclaimed...

"You heard what he said!" Veronica laughed...

"Okay! I'm eating!" I laughed as I opened my bag and took out the wedge..."

"That shit look good – what is it?"

"Chicken cheesesteak..."

"Le'me get some!" she exclaimed as Steph shook his head and left the break room...

The rest of the afternoon went better than I expected. I couldn't stop smiling. All that changed when I opened my email and saw the bereavement notice for Dana...

Happy New Year

It is with deep sorrow that we inform you of the passing of

Dana Tompkins, Director
Office of Administrative Hearings
December 24th, 2022

Wife of

Darnell Tompkins, Director
Yonkers District Office

Wake Will Be On Held Saturday, January 7th
2 p.m. – 4 p.m.
George T. Davis Funeral Home
16 Shea Place #7122
New Rochelle, NY 10805

Funeral Will Be Held On Sunday, January 8th
2 p.m. – 4 p.m.
George T. Davis Funeral Home
16 Shea Place #7122
New Rochelle, NY 10805

Condolences Can Be Sent To
Darnell Tompkins
710 Davenport Avenue, Unit 2
New Rochelle, NY 10805

"Oh my God!" Ron exclaimed as I started crying again. Veronica opened her email and she knew why I was crying. I got up from my desk and went into Steph's office...

"You saw the bereavement notice..." he sighed...

"I need to leave..." I whispered...

"Understood – I'll see you tomorrow..."

"Thank you..." I whispered as I left without saying goodbye to anyone...

"Good evening Ms. Robinson..." Robert greeted...

"Good evening Robert..."

"Have a good evening..."

"You too..." I said as I got in the elevator and went upstairs. I opened the door and as soon as I got inside, I started crying again. I missed Darnell and I wanted to call him but I also knew I needed to let him grieve and handle the arrangements for his wife. As selfish as it seemed, I wanted it to be over so I could be with him. I went to get myself a glass of moscato and I heard the notification in my phone so I picked it up and smiled when I saw I had a message from Darnell...

"Hey Chelle,

I miss you. I wish you were here to help me deal with all of this. I know that's crazy, but I wish I were in your arms right now..."

"Hey Darnell,

I wanted to call you but I know that's not a good idea. I miss you so much it hurts. I wish I could hold you and be held by you right now too.

I have this new employee that's testing me but working with Steph Richardson & Veronica is great. I'm happy and looking forward to the new chapter we're about to start. Monday can't get here fast enough..."

"I'll be counting down the hours. Once I see you, nothing and no one will keep me away from you ever again..."

"Ditto..."

I took out the moscato, poured myself a glass, and sipped it as I contemplated what I was going to make for dinner.

Excerpt from Happy New Year 2

"Ouch..."

"Ouch?!" Darnell exclaimed as he jumped up... "What's wrong?"

"I'm in pain..." I answered as I pushed myself up...

"In pain?! Where?!"

"Here..." I answered as I took his hand and put it on my right side...

"Is it my fault?" he asked out of concern...

"I don't think so..."

"So... It could be my fault?"

"Well..."

"Oh my God – I'm sorry – I didn't mean to hurt you..."

"Yes you did!" I laughed...

"Chelle! Don't say that!"

"Darnell – What did I tell you to do?" he didn't answer me right away...

"Umm... You told me to taste you..."

"And what else did I tell you to do?"

"Well... Ummm... You told me to fuck you..."

"Did you want to?"

"Hell yea I wanted to!"

"And I wanted you to..."

"Can you get up?"

"I can try..." I answered as I tried again and failed... "Ouch!"